THE LONG AWAITED
SEQUEL HAS ARRIVED

BLACK AND Ugly AS EVER

ESSENCE MAGAZINE BEST SELLING AUTHOR OF
BLACK AND UGLY AND A HUSTLERS SON

T STYLES

PUBLISHER'S NOTE:

This book is a work of fiction. Names, characters, businesses, organizations, places, events and incidents are the product of the author's imagination or are used fictionally. Any resemblance of actual persons, living or dead, events, or locales is entirely coincidental.

Library of Congress Control Number: 2008908047
ISBN: 0-9794931-6-1
ISBN 13: 978-0-9794931-6-4

Cover Design: Davida Baldwin www.oddballdsgn.com
Editor: Right Way Editorial Services
Graphics: Davida Baldwin
www.thecartelpublications.com
First Edition
Printed in the United States of America

Dedication

This is dedicated to two wonderful people.
Alphonsa Dunlap. I know the angels are laughing because of you.
This is also dedicated to my step-father Bobby Cole who also passed recently. You'll always be the LEGEND and my TRUE father.
You're both missed but I know I'll see you again.

Acknowledgments

First I'd like to thank my family (Mommy, Tina, Kavena, Kajel, D'Juan, CeCe, Angel, Charisse, Destanee, Darius, Kiara, Vincent, Aunt Paula, Dee, Carlos "30" aka Nut and anyone else I've missed). You guys put up with my absence as I struggled to put closure to a story so many people enjoyed. Thanks for loving me regardless, as much as I love you.

I'd like to thank my friends. There are so many of you so I'll try to remember as many as I can. Monica, thanks for being a true-blue friend. Forever! You're the best. Also, Mona Harris, Allyn, My Assistant Phallon Perry, you're the best. We sooo need you! Thanks for holding us down! Giovanna, Krystal, Laina, and everyone else I missed.

I'd like to thank my authors, who motivated me to get behind my pen again. Eyone Williams, Anthony Fields, K.D. Harris, V.J. Gotastory, and Tiona Dawkins, I love you guys. I'd also like to thank Jason Poole. You've become so much more to me than just an author. You're my homie and someone I consider family. I love and appreciate how you ride for me, and the Cartel, Jason. And that's real talk! I will never forget our long talks and how you always motivated me when I was down. We're kindred spirits.

I'd also like to thank Nikki Turner! Girl you are too much fun! Thanks for being real and driven. Your energy has rubbed off on me and has encouraged me to excel even higher!

And...thanks for giving me the opportunity to meet Neyo at club Love in D.C.! He's one of my favorite artists! You are the best!! I'd like to thank my Pep Squad/Street Team members. I hope you guys find pride in repping this book the way you repped the other Cartel titles.

I would be remised if I didn't thank Davida Baldwin for placing such a hot cover on this novel, and Shanice B for providing such a beautiful face.

I'd also like to thank Charisse, my inspiration for everything I do. Thanks for staying true and standing behind me through the fire. I love you.

Last but not least, I'd like to thank my fans both old and new. Your support means everything to me.

For those of you who have a hard time finding the original story, Black & Ugly, I apologize. It's unfortunate that there are individuals who hate on the success of others and like to hold them back. Contact your local libraries and me. Maybe we can think of something together. You should also know, that I do everything for you.

Love,

T. Styles

tstyles@thecartelpublications.com
www.thecartelpublications.com

What up Fam,

I haven't dropped a line to you since our debut novel, "Shyt List", but I'm back!! First off, I want to say thanks to all of you who continue to ride wit' The Cartel!! We love and appreciate the support that ya'll have and always show us. Through your support, encouragement, and love, the HEART of The Cartel continues to pump. Since I last spoke to you, our family has truly grown. We have some of the hottest authors in the street lit game on our squad puttin' out bangers and will continue to do so, for decades to come.

Now, on to business at hand, "Black and Ugly As Ever." I'm truly honored to be stampin' this one. This joint right here is cold! T. takes you on an emotional roller coaster and when the ride is over, you will definitely want to go again. I'm still trippin' off some of the shit Parade does, she a mess, but she keeps it gangsta always. So sit back and enjoy! I PROMISE you won't be disappointed! Speaking of women who keep it gangsta, in this novel, we pay homage to:

"Wahida Clark"

Wahida is one of the most vicious authors in the game. Her arsenal of novels include: "Thugs and the Women Who Love Them", "Payback is a Mutha", "Thug Matrimony", "Payback With Ya Life", "Every Thug Needs A Lady", and "Sleeping With The Enemy". Although her writing is hardcore, Wahida is humble, real, and respected. She's definitely gettin' it. It's my honor to pay tribute to her. Wahida will always have love wit' The Cartel.

Oh Yeah, if you're in the D.C./Maryland area, feel free to stop by and say what's up at our new book store. Cartel Café' & Books, located at 5011 B Indian Head Highway Oxon Hill, MD.

See ya soon!!

Charisse Washington
VP, The Cartel Publications
www.thecartelpublications.com

Quick Recap From

BLACK AND UGLY

In Black and Ugly, Sky Taylor, Parade Knight, Miss Wayne and Daffany Stans are introduced. Growing up in Hyattsville, Maryland, these friends struggle to keep their bond together.

Sky persecuted Parade for her dark skin. She believed her own light complexion gave her the advantage and didn't mind telling people to their face, including Parade. But what she didn't know was that her man Jay was sleeping with Parade behind her back.

Parade hates her complexion because of the scratches on her face, and the darkness of her skin. Despite her inner battle, she finds comfort in the curviness of her body. Miss Wayne tells her she could eliminate some of the pain she feels if she'd just take care of her acne problem, stop fighting and take pride in her beautiful skin tone. Her unattractive boyfriend Melvin, who she dumps early on, does nothing but use her sexually making her feel worse. It's not until she gets with Jay, a neighborhood dealer, behind Sky's back that she starts to gain confidence. But Jay also adds to the pressure by trying to keep her down by saying she's ugly.

One night after being with Parade an hour earlier, Jay and Sky meet up at the movies. There she sees the neighborhood kingpin Smokes and his wife who is sporting expensive jewelry. Instead of focusing on Jay, Sky does everything she can to get Smokes' attention. Smokes' shows a little interest and gets into a brief altercation with his wife when he's caught. The two leave and Sky misses her chance. Still at the movies, Sky reaches over to kiss Jay and notices he smells like

the perfume she gave Parade. She immediately suspects he's been with her instead of another girl. She questions Jay about his infidelities but doesn't let on that she thinks Parade's the culprit. After all, to Sky, Parade isn't even in her league.

The next day at the mall, Parade, Sky, Miss Wayne and Daffany, who recently discovered she was HIV positive, gets into an altercation. All because Parade believed a girl disrespected Sky. Parade holds her own and wins the battle.

In a few days, when all of the friends are at a party, Sky gets into a fight with a girl and kills her. Nobody knows Sky was involved because the fight was out of their view. The next day the murder is publicized on the news. The first person Sky confides in that she was the murderer was the same person she hurts on a regular basis, Parade. Sky tells Parade that the girl she killed in self defense was the same girl Parade fought at the mall. Parade feels guilty for getting Sky involved and vows to keep her secret.

Pretty soon Daffany and Miss Wayne suspect Sky's the one who murdered the girl. Unbeknownst to them, the woman who was murdered was not the girl at the mall. Instead she was Smokes', a cold-hearted drug dealer's wife. Smokes eventually gets a lead that Sky's involved. And to get his revenge, he hired Cannon, a hit man to find out for sure. Cannon eventually finds Parade to get closer to Sky. But he immediately becomes attracted to her beauty during the same time she starts to care about her physical appearance. With Miss Wayne's support, Parade dresses better than her friends and exhibits strong confidence. One of the first things she does is dump her boyfriend and cut off Jay. No longer able to control her, Jay becomes angry and tries to muscle Parade into a relationship. But Parade stands firm on leaving him alone, as Cannon, eventually takes up her time. Plus she doesn't want to take the risk of Sky finding out about her betrayal. The only problem is Parade doesn't know Cannon's true motives.

One day during a game of truth or dare at Miss Wayne's, Cannon's true intentions are revealed and Parade is devastated. He not only admits that he's hired to kill the person responsible for his client's wife's death, he also says that the person responsible will die that night. He never, ever mentions his client's name. Right before he attempts to place a bullet in Sky's head, someone breaks in trying to rob Miss

Wayne's apartment and Cannon is murdered. Although he wasn't able to go through with the hit, Sky is eventually killed the next day by someone else Smokes hired. Terrified, they don't go to the funeral. And eventually Smokes sends a message that if they ever said a word about Cannon or his involvement, he'd have them killed too. The only problem is no one knew who Smokes is because he never revealed himself.

A little later, Parade meets Smokes and after spending a lot of time together he eventually proposes to her. She accepts and he continues to hide his true identity from her. So Parade has no idea that he was involved in the murder of Sky. Excited about getting married, she decides to tell her friends about her engagement. Daffany, Parade and Miss Wayne all meet at the mall after not seeing each other since Sky's death. When they do, they see the girl they had believed Sky murdered. Soon it was revealed that Sky lied about everything. And when Smokes name comes up in the revelation, Parade is shocked! Parade decides to keep her relationship with him a secret from her friends. But worse of all, she still decides to go through with the engagement.

And now the story continues…

"Hearthrob Never, Black and Ugly As Ever."

-NOTORIOUS BIG

Parade Knight

THE PRESENT

Someone asked me one day, why my mother named me Parade. I ignored them. It's hard hearing the truth, that I was given my name because it took a *parade* blocking the abortion clinic to stop that bitch from terminating the pregnancy. I've been doomed since the day I was born. So it's no wonder why once again I'm sitting outside in my car at night, in Quincy Manor parking lot. Someplace I don't belong.

Drama follows me around like my shadow. I know I shouldn't be here and everything in me tells me I should go. Yet I can't seem to move my foot from the brake to the gas peddle. As I stare at my 4 carat engagement ring, I start wondering why I even believed I was ready for a commitment, when I can't get the one man I ever truly loved out my mind and off my heart.

Knock! Knock! Knock!

Shit! Jay banging on my passenger window startled me. I didn't even see him leave his building. I took a quick glimpse of myself in the mirror and placed my finger on the electronic button slowly rolling my illegally tinted window down, not sure what I'd say to him next. I feel like a whore even before I know what I'm about to do. Still, I fall victim to my one and only obsession, Jay Hernandez. My dead friend's ex-boyfriend and the

man I betrayed her with. Still, he looks better now than a year ago under the night sky.

"Why you sittin' out in the car?" he asked, in his usual raspy voice peaking through my window. He scanned inside quickly and I could tell he was checking out my fly ass ride. I never owned anything as luxurious as this. My fiancé let me drive his black on black 2008 Mercedes CL 500 like it belonged to me. And I was starting to believe that it did. Eventually Jay's eyes moved from the butter leather seats, to my body before stopping on my face.

"So why you ain't tell me you were out here?" he asked, again.

"No reason." I responded, looking down in my lap, out in front of me and than back at him. "Just thinkin'."

"Bout what? Me?" He grinned.

"Just stuff, Jay."

"Well come inside and think about *stuff*." He demanded, leaning on my car causing it to rock a little. "You shouldn't be out here this late at night."

I looked around and saw the usual suspects selling their dope and causing problems in the Manor, but they never bothered me. I guess even after I moved from around here, not a lot has changed.

"I can't come in," I whispered. "You know that."

"You can't or you don't want to?"

"I'm not sure," I hunched my shoulders allowing them to fall just as quickly.

"But I want you to," he said sincerely. "That's why you're here, to be with me."

Is this the same man that called me black and ugly every time he laid eyes on me back in the day? And if so, why is he being so nice? Even now I'm sitting here counting down the minutes before he reminds me of the past by calling me a bitch and demanding that I get on my knees and suck his dick. I was his

whore. A dirty washrag that he used and threw away.

And then he says, "And you look sexy as shit tonight, shawty."

Did he just say what I think he did? I use to hope he'd say things like that to me. Only if he knew it took me three hours to find the right outfit to wear. I finally settled on a tight pair of Seven blue jeans, and a black Bebe top with the word in rhinestones over my right breast. My black hair lay flat on my shoulders and my makeup was flawless.

"Whatever, Jay. I don't hardly look sexy," I frowned, sitting back into my car seat. My hands rested firmly on my wood grain steering wheel. "So stop talkin' like that." I unconsciously adjusted my hair to be sure it was neat, something Sky had always done when men were around.

"I'm serious, Parade. You look *real* sexy, and you know I don't say shit I don't mean." *Silence*. "So come inside," he continued. "We have a lot of catchin' up to do."

"Jay, I'm engaged." I reminded him, flashing my ring. I saw the brightness from the street light catch its glow and shine against his face causing him to squint. "You know I can't do that."

"Fuck that nigga and fuck that ring! If you cared about either of 'em, you wouldn't even be around here!" he yelled, tapping the top of my car. "I knew you before he even knew you were alive. Or did you forget?"

"Come on, Jay," I exhaled, tempted to pull off, my car still in drive and foot still on the brake. "Please don't do this right now. I don't even know why I came."

"Me either." He was cold and stood up straight causing my car to rock again. The look in his eyes reminded me that he still felt something for me, even if he didn't know what it was. He backed away and I was able to see what he was wearing. He was sportin' a red *Blac Label* shirt, and blue *Rock and Republic* jeans. His hair was cut lower than usual but I could still see the soft curls in it that use to be longer, compliments of his black and Spanish heritage. “If you don’t wanna be here, I’m not keepin’ you. Keep it movin’.”

Why is he always so cold? This man turns on and off like running water.

“But I *do* wanna be here.” I blurted out, wishing I could take it back, placing my car in park. “You know that.”

“Then check it,” he said, looking behind my car and then at me. “If you hang out wit’ me this weekend, I’ll get you out of somethin’ that’s gettin’ ready to go down.”

“What?” I asked, confused at his request.

“Give me your answer quick.” I noticed a set of headlights shining brightly in my rearview mirror. I was blinded and couldn’t see who was coming. Plus I was so busy focusing on Jay’s sly smile that I couldn’t give him an answer.

“Duck down and don’t lift up,” Was what he said next. And than he yelled, “Is that my nigga, Zeeway?!” He called out as the car pulled in the parking space on the left of me. Jay walked directly between our cars blocking my view. “What’s good?” he gave him some dap.

As they spoke I thought about the name he said. *Zeeway*. He was one of Smokes best friends who just got out after doing a five year bid in Smoke’s name. He always talked about how when he got out, he’d look after him for eating time that rightfully belonged to him.

Although Zeeway never saw me, I knew we would eventually meet, I just hoped it wouldn’t be like this. I would have a tough time explaining to Smokes why I was sitting outside of Jay’s building at Quincy Manor Apartments, when I was *his* fiancé.

“Ain’t nothin’, yo,” Zeeway responded. “Dem your peoples?” he asked, his voice reflecting loudly in my direction.

I stooped down lower. I knew he couldn’t see me but I was sure he saw my shoulder length hair. I would have to change

it soon. I was tempted to roll up my window knowing I could conceal myself behind its darkness, but that would've been too hot and too obvious. Zeeway would've known I was trying to hide something then.

"Naw." Jay laughed. "She's just stoppin' through."

"Then why she hidin'?" He was being too nosey for my taste. "I been locked up for a minute and I'm tryin' to see a pretty face."

What difference does it make? Pull the fuck off!

"Cuz she ain't here for you man," Jay laughed. "What's up, nigga? How long you been out?" He asked, skipping the subject.

"A nigga fresh off the block today. And you know me," he laughed. "I'm already tryin' to slide into somethin' soft before I check a few dudes out about my bread." I wasn't positive but I had a feeling the comment about slidin' into something soft was meant for me.

"I heard that! Who you checkin' first?"

"Smokes for one," he said, in a devious tone. "Don't get me wrong, he looked after my books while I was in, but that wasn't enough for the five years I ate for him, feel me?"

"I heard that," Jay responded. "Hold on for a sec." Jay interrupted their conversation to turn toward me.

Hearing my fiancé's name caused me to gasp for breath. I couldn't help but wonder if the name drop was deliberate. Did he want me to know that he knew who I was? I was starting to feel faint.

Jay was now back at my window and said, "Look...you gonna hook up wit' me or do I have to make things hot for you?" he asked, in a low voice his head half way in my car. I was happy his body was blocking my face but uneasy that Zeeway's attention was now directed at me and Smoke's car.

"I can't." I attempted to continue to hide from Zeeway. "Get rid of him!"

"Hey, Zee," Jay said, turning around cutting me off almost revealing my identity. "You want to meet my friend?"

"Hell yeah!" he replied.

"Okay!" I grabbed his hand. "When do you wanna hook up?"

"Be here tomorrow night at 8:00, Parade. And don't be bullshittin' me."

"Alright, Jay." I was defeated. "I'll be here."

"And don't be late eitha!"

"Alright," I repeated. "Just get rid of his ass!"

He smiled and turned around to lose Zeeway. I know I sound and look crazy right now. I even know what you're thinking. But let me take you back a little and tell you my story. *The whole story*. I'm gonna tell you how I ran into Jay again a month ago, after not seeing him for a year. I'm also going to tell you why I'm outside of his apartment building instead of being at home with my fiancé.

So grab a seat because my life is far from boring. And trust me, some of the things that happened will trip you out, but one thing I promise you, it's all true.

Miss Wayne

A YEAR EARLIER

Whatever Miss Parade got to tell me betta be good. It took me two weeks to get Shonda to treat and color my wig only for me to cancel! And to top it all off, I got a blind date with this nigga name Keith in forty minutes and I didn't even get a chance to tape down my goodies. I'm liable to scare the poor man to death with the rocks I got dangling between my legs right now.

I walked carefully into *Cactus Willies*, an all you can eat spot in Baltimore County looking for Parade and Daffany. And outside of smuggling a bag of knots between my legs, I looked fierce! My red pumps clicked against the porcelain floors like a soft drum as I moved. I was *Swaga-Licious*! I was killing them with the black pants, and velvet red shirt.

I was in there five seconds when I saw Miss Parade and Miss Daffany sitting a few feet over from the entrance. I was walking in their direction when I heard, "Welcome to Cactus Willies," a cute little white girl smiled from behind the counter. "How can I help you?" She continued, staring at my family jewels.

Clearing my throat I said, "Excuse me, sweetheart, my face is up here."

"Oh…I'm sorry, sir," she apologized, stealing one last

look. "What can I do for you?" Her face was beet red with embarrassment.

"I'm meetin' some friends here and I see them over there." I responded, flashing one last smile at her. "So there's no need to trouble yourself with me, I'll just be a second." I gently placed my hand over hers before removing it slowly.

As I walked toward the table again she yelled, "You still have to pay, sir!"

I stopped dead in my tracks, turned around and said, "Maybe you didn't hear me, precious," I frowned, clutching the collar on my blouse due to her rude outburst. "They're right over there and I'm not going to eat. You can sit with me if you don't believe me, darling. As you can see," I continued, rubbing my hand over my legs and stomach. "One meal and these black stretch Lycra pants are liable to split and drop to the floor."

I giggled.

She didn't.

"I understand, sir," she explained. "But I can't let you in without paying. I'll get in trouble."

To shoosh this little girl I grabbed twenty dollars out of my red hobo style purse slammed it on the counter and switched my tiny ass toward the table.

Once there I said, "This betta be good, girl." I advised, after being humiliated by Raggedy Ann. I sat in the seat, crossed my legs and waited anxiously for the *T* (talk). "What's the deal?"

"As you both know, I'm getting married." She said, carefully looking at Daffany and then back at me. "But what you don't know is who I'm marrying."

There was twenty seconds of uncomfortable silence.

"Go 'head, chile," I interjected, no longer able to contain my composure. "What's his name? Where's he from? And how big is his dick?"

"I'm gonna tell you," she said softly, slightly uncomfortable. She grabbed the cup filled with ice water off the table,

drank it while looking at us from the bottom of the wet glass. When it was all gone she said, "This is hard for me."

"Parade," Daffany said, stroking her hand before gripping it lovingly. "We're your friends. With everything we have going on in our own lives we would be crazy for judging you. Just keep it real with us and tell us what you've been hiding. Is it a girl?"

"No!" she laughed. "You know I'm on dick too hard," she continued. "But it's like this," she said, smiling gingerly, moving in closer, "Sky killed my new fiancé's wife."

"Sky killed your new fiancé's wife? What?" Miss Daffany said, looking at me and then at Parade for clarification. "I'm confused."

You don't understand. Sky was our best friend. We grew up together and just recently she was murdered viciously. So the fact that she was saying she was marrying Sky's killer was a hot ass mess and didn't make much sense.

"I'm marrying the man that had Sky murdered."

Silence.

"Come again." I raised my right brow. "Because I know I didn't hear what I think I heard. On second thought," I advised pushing my chair back a few inches to stand up. "Hold that thought. I have to get something to eat first." Nothing does a brain better than some carbs, and after what I just heard, I'm gonna need two plates full.

After excusing myself, I loaded my plate with fried chicken, mac and cheese, greens, fried shrimp, banana pudding, honey buttered rolls, and then I grabbed a diet coke to watch my calories. I know I said I wasn't gonna eat but I say a lot of shit I don't mean so you gonna have to forgive me right now. Because this is too crazy and I can't believe I heard what I *thought* Parade said. *I'm marrying the man that had Sky murdered.* Her words echoed over and over in my mind.

When I returned Miss Daffany was staring at Parade as if she wanted to scratch her eyeballs out. I can't say I blame her. I stuffed my face with fried chicken and took two bites of Mac and cheese. When I thought about what Miss Parade said again, I grabbed a butter roll and chewed half of it too. I felt my stomach swelling by the bite and I was starting to feel uncomfortable in my clothes. Now I'm really pissed and Parade's to blame for me bustin' out of my gear. Now I'll have to go home and get dressed before meetin' my new baby daddy, Keith.

Parade and Daffany both looked at me wanting me to break the silence. Ever since I've known them, I've been daddy, mommy and every other dysfunctional family member you could think of. And even after Sky's murder, nothing has changed. I swallowed the food in my mouth, pat the corners of my lips with a napkin and decided to be short and sweet with my feelings about all of this.

"What the hell you mean you marrying Sky's killer?!" A few people turned around looking at me and I said, "And what the hell are ya'll lookin' at?!" When they proceeded to mind their own business I faced Miss Parade awaiting her answer.

"I know it seems crazy, but I swear I didn't know he was involved in any of this shit until it was too late! It wasn't until I saw the girl Sky supposedly killed in the mall that I put one and one together! Hell she knew more about Smokes than I did at the time."

You see, me…Miss Daffany, Miss Parade and Miss Sky were held at gunpoint by a hired killer because Miss Sky murdered Smoke's wife at a party. But, Miss Sky being the character that she was before she died lied to Parade and told her it was the girl Parade had beef with at the mall. Miss Sky said she had to kill the girl in self defense. You had to be in my life beforehand to get the full story.

"Parade, this don't make no damn sense!" Miss Daffany added, wiping her hands down her face before gripping her arms. "Sky had her problems but she was still our best friend. I mean… must you fuck all of her men?"

"Daffany, please," Miss Parade rolled her eyes as she pushed a little back from the table. "You talkin' about must I fuck all of her men when you slept with every one of our men too!"

"What?" Miss Daffany yelled leaping from her seat. It was the first time I saw what she was wearing, a dingy white t-shirt, blue jeans and run over tennis shoes.

"You heard me Daffany! You think I don't know you been fuckin' my ex-boyfriend Melvin for the longest? When you knew I was with him? What if I would've gotten that AIDS shit you spreadin' around?"

"Parade, don't do this!" I yelled. Both of them ignored me.

"Like you gave a fuck about Melvin!" Daffany responded, still in shock by Parade's comment. "I did you a fuckin favor! Consider yourself lucky! But at least I didn't fuck the man who sent our best friend to her grave!"

"Excuse me," an older white lady with wrinkles sitting at the table across from us interrupted. "But can you all keep it down please?"

"Can you still suck a dick?" I asked, as I waited for her response.

She gripped her mouth and looked to the older gentlemen at the table with her.

"Don't look at me. I told you to mind your own old business." He told her focusing back on his meal.

I directed my attention back to Parade and Daffany and they didn't miss a beat. They continued to go at each other's throat.

"At least I didn't almost give her AIDS like you did me!" Miss Parade retaliated.

"Hold up ya'll! This is getting too personal." I advised. "Now Miss Parade, what I think Miss Daffany is tryin' to say is that you're not dating but marrying somebody who sent us through a lot of shit recently. Don't forget that hit man he hired

to kill Miss Sky almost killed us too."

"No, what I'm sayin' is that Parade has lost her fuckin' mind!" Daffany corrected me. "All your life you played the victim by believing you were so ugly, you had to settle for the first thing that came along. Just because you're dark-skinned. Well I'm sick of having a pity party for you and I'm sick of your bullshit! That shit ends today! I feel like kickin' your ass right now."

"You can try it!" Miss Parade said, jumping up removing her earrings next. "Cuz I'll lay your ass flat on your back!"

Miss Daffany softened her scowl and backed down. We all knew Miss Parade could kick her ass in her sleep. I also knew that Miss Daffany must've been real mad to challenge her.

"Hold up now!" I stood up knocking the table with my hips and causing all of the food and drink to hit the floor. When the little white girl saw the table topple over, she covered her mouth and ran to the back. I guess to get a manager or somethin'. "Shit! Look what ya'll made me do!"

Neither one of them made any attempts to help with the mess.

"Let's not do this, ya'll. We've been friends far too long," I continued, eyeing the mess and the crowd that was watching us. "Miss Sky wouldn't want us fighting like this!"

"Fuck Parade, Miss Wayne!" Miss Daffany yelled, pointing her finger toward Miss Parade. "She's nobody's friend and Sky probably rollin' over in her grave eight times behind this shit."

"Girl, you got five seconds to get your finger out of my fuckin' face before I break it off!"

Miss Daffany removed her finger quick. "You think just because you're dark you can do whatever you want as an excuse! I'm tired of it! If you marry him, Parade I swear to God I'll never talk to you again and you can consider our friendship over!"

There was five seconds of silence before Miss Parade said, "I guess we weren't friends to begin with! Never was!"

Miss Daffany took one look at her and ran out of the restaurant crying. I tried to grab her wrist but she shook me off. Then I was trying to calm Miss Parade down when I saw the hysterical white girl walking in our direction with a black piece of man candy in slacks and a dress shirt.

"We're going to have to ask you both to leave." He said, as kindly as possible.

"I'm leaving anyway!" Miss Parade said grabbing her black and gold purse. Then she put back on her earrings. "Miss Wayne, if you want to reach me, you know where I be, but I *am* gonna marry him. He loves me and I need him. It's as simple as that!" With that she was gone leaving me alone with these asses.

All I could say to the employees was, "Can I have a doggie bag?"

Daffany

I just need something to relax, that's it. If I can just calm down, maybe then I'll understand why Parade would go as far as she is by marrying a murderer! Let's be real! What is she thinkin'?! And how does she know he won't kill her if she gets him wrong? Let's not forget, he was the same man that vowed to kill us all if we *ever* revealed that he had somethin' to do with our best friend Sky's death! What's to stop him from acting on it now? I don't recall him giving us an expiration period on his death threat! I know you look at me and see everything the world despises…a light-skin-Chinese and black-lookin'-whore on drugs with AIDS, but at least I accept who I am. I wish I could say the same for Parade.

I pull up into my parking lot at Quincy Manor apartments scanning the dark spaces for the one man that could make my problems go away. I saw a few neighborhood dealers but nobody I trusted. *Where's Kyte?* I parked my black Civic in front of my apartment building and rummaged through my glove compartment for spare change. I stopped when I realized I played this game over and over right before I was about to cop. I almost never found any money. As usual, I'll have to rely on my pussy to get me what I need. It's the one thing that has never failed me.

Before jumping out of my car, I adjusted the rearview mirror so I could see in it, then I put a glob of spit in my hand, and smoothed the few straggly pieces of loose hair hanging from my ponytail hoping they'd stay in place. Next I tucked my white

t-shirt in my blue jeans. When I was comfortable enough with my look, I hopped out of my car and scanned the grounds for my prey. It was a comfortable summer night which meant everybody would be out grindin'. But where is Kyte? He's usually out here. I saw a few dudes and decided to settle on Gee instead to cop from, since he was the only one I never got with sexually.

"Hey, Gee," I smiled, trying to figure out if he was down for what I needed done. I put my hands on my hips and lowered my eyes. My sex appeal was in full mode and I know he was feelin' me. "You seen Kyte, baby?"

"Naw." He was short and looked everywhere else but at me.

"Well forget Kyte." I persisted, rubbing my hand on his shoulder. "I wanna know how you doin'?"

"Get your, crackhead ass out of my face befo I bust yo shit wide open!" He screamed, pushing me off of him. "I can't stand when ya'll, mothafuckas think ya'll sexy when, ya'll not."

"I'm not on crack."

"You on somethin'."

"Whateva. It's not that deep, Gee. I was just fuckin' wit you anyway." I continued walking away before things progressed.

"Yeah whateva you, raggedy bitch! You ain't nothin' but a, washed up ass whore!"

Back in the day his comment would've hurt me. But the truth was, I was a whore…with AIDS. I can either dwell on it or not, and I chose not too. Anyway he was just grandstandin' in front of his crew. If we were out here alone, we would've been behind the building with his dick in my mouth by now.

When I spotted Tywon, another dealer, I knew he'd be down for whatever. He's only nineteen and thinks with one thing and one thing only, his dick. I've been with him before. The only bad part about Ty is that he likes it rougher than I can stand sometimes. He likes to fuck me roughly in my ass and bite my shoulders almost drawing blood. I know it sounds fucked up but he never broke the skin and we always used condoms. I ain't tryin' to spread this shit around…just get high. But as desperate as I am, I'm willing to do whatever.

He was leaning against the brick building next to mine but stood up straight when he saw me walk in his direction. His dark chocolate skin and bright white teeth were flawless. He looked good in his blue jeans and plain white T. I sashayed over toward him swaying my hips from left to right.

"Hey, Ty. You wanna have some fun with me tonight?"

"It depends," he smiled back unconsciously checking his surroundings as most hustlers do when they're on the grind. But this time unlike with Gee, his focus did return to me.

"On what?"

"It depends on what you consider fun," he asked, looking at me before licking his lips.

"I think you know what I consider fun since we've played together many times before. So let's not even go there."

"And what do I owe this offer?"

"Nothin…," I lied. "Except a little piece of candy."

He frowned and asked, "When you gonna start gettin' down like the big girls and leave that E alone?"

"What are you talkin' about?" I asked, turning up my nose.

"I'm askin' when you gonna stop poppin' pills and raise your game?" he winked; taking one last look around him before he gently grabbed my forearm and pulled me closer. Reaching down on the stoop, he removed a lose brick in the concrete and pulled out a tiny Ziploc bag filled with a hard yellow substance. I was so close to him that only he and I could see what he had in his hands. My heart began to beat quickly because I knew exactly what he was saying now. It was the same shit that had my mother running around here lookin' a mess. Heroin. I vowed to never go that far and I didn't see any reason in starting now. As

far as I was concerned, the E was enough for me. As if he could read my mind he whispered in my ear. "Don't you want to float away whenever you get ready without catchin' a plane?" His voice was deep, borderline erotic. The heat from his breath brushed my ear. "Don't you wanna be able to have a full body orgasm whenever you want to?" As if I wasn't already captivated, he pulled me so close that not even air could pass between us. "Don't you want to get the fuck away from reality?"

Out of everything he said, I listened to his last question the most. It struck home. I do want to escape my life. And if I wasn't scared, I would've killed myself along time ago. I was already walking around half dead, but after Sky's death, I became colder.

"And how much you gonna charge me if I do decide to go there?"

"The first ones on me."

His offer was sounding better and better. Something told me to run, but my feet remained planted.

"Why you procrastinatin'?! You gonna do it or not cause I got payin' customers who woulda accepted my offer a long time ago?" he quickly turned from the nice pusher man to one of these young dumb ass drug dealers.

I was about to give my answer until, "Daffany!" a familiar voice called from behind me. "Let me holla at you for a sec."

When I turned around I saw Jay walking in my direction. I frowned, my face and said, "Give me a minute." I didn't want him to overhear that I was considerin' takin' things to the next level with my habit.

Jay yelled, "Let me holla at you now!"

"Damn, Jay!" Ty laughed, raising his arms and tilting his head slightly. "We were handlin' business ova here."

"That's why I want to talk to her now. Don't worry lil nigga. I got you later."

Ty took one look at me and then at him and said,

"Wheneva you ready, you know where to find me."

"But I'm ready now."

He looked at Jay again for the okay but with his hands, Jay told him to cut things short with me. I was angry just thinkin' about how he was getting ready to fuck my shit up.

"Naw...just get up with me lada." He walked off.

These dealers around here respected Jay too much.

I was looking at my chance at a high walk away, when I turned around and saw Jay standing before me. Even though he had gotten with Parade back in the day, everything about him reminded me of Sky and I began to feel worst.

"What do you want, Jay?" I asked, as I rolled my eyes.

"First off…what's wit the attitude?"

"I was taken care of somethin' about a job and you messed it up!" I placed my hands on my hips.

"So you was talkin' to a dealer about a job, huh?"

"Yeah…I needed some money to catch the bus because I start my new job tomorrow and he was gonna give it to me."

"Why would you do that when you have a car, Daffany?" He reminded me.

"Jay, what's up?" I yelled, embarrassed I was caught in a lie. All I knew was that I needed to get high and I needed to get high quick.

"I'ma cut to the chase," he said, smoothing his invisible beard with his right hand. "Where's your girl?"

I knew he was getting ready to ask me about that bitch! That's why I wasn't even tryin' to hear him when he opened his mouth.

"I don't know. I'm not her keeper." I responded, walking away.

"You are if I say you are." He said confidently. When I turned around he showed me a closed fist with the tip of a C note peaking through.

I walked toward him. Slowly, but anxiously as if that was

possible.

"What I gotta do?"

"You gotta call Parade for me and tell her to meet you somewhere."

"No."

"Aight…let me know how long it takes you to get half of what I'm 'bout to give you tonight. I hear you had that good shit at one time. But niggas sayin' you washed up now," he said referring to my pussy. "So good luck." He walked away and I let down my guards. Why give away pussy when he was gonna hook me up right now.

"Okay!"

"Okay what?" he responded turning back around.

"Okay I'll do it."

"You sure?" he asked sarcastically. "Cause I don't want you to do nothin' you don't want to do."

"I said I'll do it," I continued, reaching for the money.

"Hold up," he extended his hand before him taking the money away. "I want you to tell her to meet you out here tonight."

"She not gonna do it because we just had a fight."

Jay looked toward the ground as if he was trying to think and then said, "Aight, tell her to meet you at the IHOP on Bladensburg road. Tell her you need to talk and that you were sorry about whateva bullshit ya'll was beefin about."

The mere thought of apologizing made my stomach churn.

"Aight gimme the money."

"Not until you call her."

"I will when I get in the house."

"I'm not fuckin' wit you, do it now or the deal is off." He handed me his silver Blackberry.

I dialed her number disgusted by the whole idea. Whatever he got to say to her I sure hope it's worth it.

"And, Daffany," he interrupted, stopping the call. "You don't want to fuck wit' that shit."

"What shit?"

"That bullshit you was 'bout to cop from Ty. It ain't for you, shawty."

Silence.

Why did he care if I was thinkin' about fucking with heroin? It was my business not his. Still, a part of me felt good that he even cared and the other part said he needed to mind his business and let me run my life. Whatever life I had left.

Parade

I gripped onto the edge of the shelf in the tiny pantry closet trying to handle Smoke's swift strokes against my ass cheeks. Light peeking under the doorway allowed me to see his pants hanging down by his ankles and my toes spread against the cream porcelain floor. As big as this house was, Smokes insisted on fucking me everywhere else but in the bedroom. His reason? As long as we were together he'd always make it hot. And as good as this bald headed mothafucka treated me, anything he wanted I was down for.

"Damn, ma!! This pussy is the bomb! Squeeze them walls again." He demanded.

I complied.

"Squeeze that thang tighter."

I tightened up more.

"That feel better, but you gotta work on that shit," he continued, pumping in and out of me.

Sometimes he treated me like I was in training when we made love and I hated it.

"That pussy smells good though," he continued, as he took his finger, rubbed it over my clit and smelled it. He loved the smell of pussy. "Why that shit smell so good?"

"Cause nobody hittin' this but you, daddy and I keep it clean." I responded, backing up. I liked when he wanted it on the spontaneous tip minus the lessons on how to work it. Besides, I been working my shit for years and if there was one thing I knew

how to do, fucking was it. Just so long as he didn't want it the *wet* way. I'll explain that shit later.

"You betta know that's right," he continued, as he banged me against the canned green beans causing one of them to fall to the floor, missing my foot by inches. None of that stopped his purpose, busting a nut inside of me.

Since the day we talked about marriage, he had a vision. What was it? Me walking down the aisle pregnant with his baby girl. He always said that when he had another child and wife he wanted to marry both of them at the alter. Not only did he want me to be pregnant ruining any chances of me having fun on *our* wedding day, he also wanted me to give him a daughter. Like I had the power to pick the baby's sex. The only thing was, when I tried to stop the birth control pills I was taking, he would continuously tell me that now was not the right time. It was like he was saying two different things.

"Shit!" He grabbed my ponytail and used it for leverage. His thickness was first class and I never been with a man his size before. I could feel his sweat fall against my back making my baby-t moist.

"I love you, ma."

"I love you too, daddy!"

"Ain't you glad I wifed you?"

"Yes, daddy! You saved me." He loved when I talked to him like that. It brought him on quicker and I was willing to say anything to help get him there. I had gotten mine fifteen minutes ago and was starting to get cramps in this awkward position. My fiancé was anything but a two minute brother. He almost climaxed until he heard my phone ring.

"Hold up, baby!" he was growing harder and harder. "I'm almost there."

"Beat that shit, baby! Beat that pussy up!" The slaps of his balls against my ass resonated throughout the closet. It's a good thing Lil Damian, his son, was away at his mother's house.

"You, sexy mothafucka what you think I'm doin', huh?" he asked, as his sweat dripped on my lower back.

"That's right, baby! Handle it!"

I hoped he was able to ignore the ring tone sound of *Mirror* by Neyo playing on my phone.

"Awwwwww shiiitttt!!!" he yelled.

I guess he was able to tune it out after all. He squeezed my waist hard and pushed all of his creamy load inside of me. A tingly sensation overwhelmed my belly. I loved being able to please him.

He kissed my shoulder and pulled out of me. When we were done, he opened the door and a gust of air came rushing in. It was hot in the tiny closet so the breeze was welcoming. He pulled up his pants and helped me with my panties, kissing my butt cheeks before placing them all the way on.

"Who callin' you in the middle of the night?" he asked, as he sat on the stool at the black marble breakfast nook in our kitchen. "They all most fucked me up."

"I don't know, baby. You want something to eat?" I asked, going directly for the cabinets. The question was rhetorical cause he always wanted to eat after we fucked.

"Yeah…warm me up some leftovers."

"Got it, baby."

"So you gonna call them back or what?" He persisted, as he wiped the sweat off of his head with a paper towel.

Let me tell you about my man. In the back of his mind he thinks I'm steppin' out on him. He might not say it, but he's definitely thinkin' it. I would be a fool for cheating on him. I live in a beautiful home in a quiet residential area. I have more clothes in my closet than I can wear. I can shop at Tiffanys, Saks and Nieman & Marcus without flipping over tags, and I feel sexier than I ever did in my life, despite this dark skin that has plagued me since I was born. I was living the glamorous life.

"I don't even know who it was, baby," I tell him as I

remove three Tupperware containers filled with barbeque ribs, mac and cheese, and collard greens from the fridge. "I'm tendin' to my man right now."

"Is that right?" he smiled.

"You want to go another round and ask me that question again?"

"You got it," he winked. "I can't fuck wit it right now. You tryna put a nigga in a coma." Just when he said that his phone rang and Lil' Wayne's *Mr. Carter* blasted as his ring tone. "Speak on it." He yelled into the receiver. Most people said hello but not my man. "Nigga, what you want?" he asked, standing up moving to the fridge grabbing a beer. "What you mean ya'll out? You got the rest of my money yet?"

Silence.

"Well bring that shit and meet me at my house in forty minutes! And, Silver…don't be late."

When I placed his warmed up food on the nook in front of him, he wrapped his arm around my waist and whispered, "Go put some clothes on." I was getting ready to do as he said when he pulled me back and said, "And look cute too. Wear that red joint I picked up for you yesterday."

"Okay," I smiled slightly embarrassed at how he insisted on dressing me. I know I *was* a bottom of the todem pole bitch, but I believe my game has raised a little since we got together. I know what to wear and how to look. I subscribed to 9 magazines to keep up with the latest fashions. "You want anything else before I get dressed?" I forced out.

"Naw."

With that he made another call. I grabbed my phone and noticed the missed call I got when Smokes was banging my back out was blocked but I had a voicemail. I dialed my mailbox and waited for the message. My heart dropped when I heard Daffany's voice.

Parade, its Daffany. I'm sorry about what happened ear-

lier today. We need to talk cuz I hate beefin' with you. When you get this message I'll be at the IHOP in Bladensburg. I know its last minute but I really need to talk to you. Come see me. Please.

Whoa! I can't believe she actually reached out. Daffany is more stubborn than me. When she holds a grudge she never comes around. I'm not gonna lie, hearing her voice and apology made me feel better because I'd been thinkin' about her and our friendship being over ever since I left her earlier.

I rushed to our bathroom, shut the door and freshened up real quick. Smokes was off the phone roaming around the house which meant Silver's ass was on his way. I hated looking at him knowing he was Markee's brother. And I was secretly happy that Jay had his ass murdered for raping his cousin.

Knock. Knock. Knock.

"Come in, baby." I hollered, as I smoothed the toner on my face. Lately whenever I washed my face and used my toner, I noticed the smell was stronger than normal. Smokes came in and wrapped his arms around my waist and looked at me through the mirror.

"I didn't mean to brush you off." His breath smelled of barbeque sauce. "Silver's bitch ass is on the way. Seems like this nigga can't even hold his dick without my direction," he continued, rocking me lightly. "I just like to make sure my wife is on point at all times."

"We're not married yet," I joked, washing the cleaner off my face.

"You belong to me now." He was serious but maintained a smile. "And I'd do anything for you."

"I know honey."

"Will you do anything for me? Anything? Even if it means death?"

Silence.

Hoping things would never get that far I said, "Anything, baby. You can count on me to come through. I just can't do it tonight," I giggled. "Daffany just called and wants to hook up. We meetin' at the IHOP."

"I thought ya'll weren't talkin'?"

"I know but she called me and said she wanted to apologize. We been friends too long to keep up shit wit' each other."

"Yeah whateva. Call me when you get there."

"I will." I turned around to kiss his lips. "I love you."

"You know I'm feelin' you too." He smiled rubbing the back of his hand on my face. "Parade, you keepin' the windows rolled up when you out?"

"Sometimes why?"

"Cuz you gettin' a little darker. I don't want the sun messin' up my baby's beautiful complexion."

That hurt.

"I'll be mindful in the future, Smokes."

"Don't be mad, Melanie. I'm just lookin' out that's all."

Silence.

"Parade."

"Parade what?" He sounded confused, but I wasn't.

"My name is Parade."

"I know what your name is." He responded defensively.

"You called me Melanie again, baby."

"Stop trippin'," he said going for the door. "I know what I said. Just make sure you call me when you get there." He walked out the door.

He's called me his wife's name at least three times since we've been together. Sometimes I wonder if he's trying to replace her using me. What scares me the most is not that he thinks I'm her sometimes, it's that I don't care.

I made it to IHOP an hour after Daffany called me. I didn't see her car anywhere. I looked overdressed with my red and green Gucci short set. But fuck it! Since I'm here I might as well grab a bite to eat.

After being seated by a little white girl I decided to order the Southwestern Omelette and a glass of water. I checked my watch one last time to see how long it had been since Daffany called. Exactly two hours passed. I was getting heated just thinking that she left me hanging.

"Anything else, mam?" the waitress asked, dropping my plate off.

"No." I smiled. "I'm fine."

When she left I realized she forgot my water. I turned around to remind her but she was already in the back. When I turned around to eat, Jay was sitting in the seat in front of me.

"What's up, Parade?" his curly hair was neatly shaped. The black t-shirt he wore showcased his platinum chain beautifully. The cologne he wore was an aphrodisiac. I'm so glad I wore this outfit. I knew I was looking hot! And he looked so fuckin' sexy.

"What are you doing here, Jay?" I asked, fiddling around with my omelet.

"I'm here to pick up my carryout order." He fell back against the booth style seat.

"Well I'm waitin' on Daffany so you gotta leave."

"I'll wait until she gets here." I wanted to say no but my heart raced like it did every time I saw him. "So how you been?"

"I'm good," I responded slowly. "Just trying to settle in that's all."

"I heard that. So how's life?"

"Why, Jay?" I asked, dropping the fork against my plate looking into his eyes briefly.

"Cause I want to know."

"You never cared before."

"Well I care now. So tell me what's good wit you.""

"I'm getting married." I decided to let it right out. He was gonna find out anyway.

And instead of him being upset he said, “Congratulations.”

“Thank you.” I responded, disappointed that I didn’t get a better reaction from him.

“So who’s the lucky, bamma?”

“Smokes.”

“Smokes?” He repeated surprised. He sat up straight, looked around and back at me. “You sure you know what you gettin’ into fuckin’ wit him?” he whispered. “That nigga’s a straight killa.”

“You sound like you on his nuts.”

The lines in his forehead got deeper and I knew I pushed my limits with that comment.

“I’ma ignore that shit you just said cause you my, shawty,” he announced. “I just know what type of shit he be on. And didn’t he have somethin’ to do with Sky gettin’ killed?”

I looked around hoping no one heard him and said, “What does that supposed to mean?”

“It means you fuckin’ wit somebody off your level. A straight murderer. I’m just lookin’ out that’s all.”

“Off my level? Lets not forget I snagged your ass!” I shot back.

Silence.

“Aight…calm down, Parade. I’m just lookin’ out for you. You do what you want to for real,” he backed down although it was clear he was bothered.

“It doesn’t matter, Jay. I’m just waitin’ on Daffany so you can excuse yourself.”

“She ain’t comin’.”

I looked at him and squinted my eyes. “What you mean she ain’t comin’?”

“She not comin’,” he repeated. “I saw her at the Manor earlier kickin’ it with some nigga.”

“Well I’m still waitin’. So bye, Jay.”

"Parade, I don't want you to marry that mothafucka."

My heart felt like it escaped my body with his words. I was confused and scared all together. You don't understand, I use to worship the ground he walked on. And he treated me like I was lower than life. Dealin' with him hurt but I got use to it. You know, like getting your eyebrows waxed. After while, it just doesn't hurt anymore.

"What you say, Jay?"

"I said I don't want you to marry him, Parade. Now we had our problems, and I know it's fucked up that I use to fuck wit' Sky considerin' ya'll were friends, but I wasn't feelin' her nowhere near how I'm feelin' you. And I told her that right before she died. I told her how much you meant to me. So I ain't out here tryin' to get wit' you because she's gone. I'm feelin' you. I always did."

"You just talkin' shit." I told him trying not to cry. I hated hearing about Sky and the fact that she ain't here no more. And I hated hearing how I betrayed our friendship when she was alive. But Sky was so mean to me. So cold. And I learned after her death, that she wasn't even honest.

"Parade, I'm serious. I know it's fucked up, but when I heard that you was gettin' married today it blew me . I just didn't know who it was wit' But I'm bein' real wit' you. I want you back."

"Hold up, what you mean when you heard today I was gettin' married?" I pushed the water cup from in front of me.

"I asked Daffany to get you out here for me." He sat back in the chair.

"What?! This was a set up? That bitch was neva comin'?"

"No. She did it cuase I paid her."

"Fuck this shit!" I yelled, getting up reaching for my purse. "I'm outta here."

I saw Jay drop a one hundred dollar bill on the table and run behind me. Once at my car he pushed me up against it. The back of my shirt was raised slightly and I felt the cold car against my skin.

"Stop playin' games with me, Parade! You gonna have me kill this muvfuka' for gettin' in my way! Plus you still love me."

"Still love you! Neva that!" I screamed unable to look at him or push him away. His presence made me weak.

"Stop bullshitin' wit' ya self, Shawty!? You was on my nuts way before I even knew you were alive!"

I smacked the fuck out of him and he grabbed my hands, pulled me to him and kissed my lips. We probably looked like freaks outside in the parking lot on my car. I ran my fingers through his hair and his hands moved up my blouse. My nipples became erect in his hands.

"Tell me you don't want me and I'll go," He passionately kissed my neck.

"I can't do that because I do want you."

"Leave that nigga, Parade. Leave his ass."

"I…I….don't know." I told him in between his kisses. I want him so bad right now I can't hardly think about my loyalty to Smokes. "Hold on," I told him. "Let's get in the car. I don't want anybody he knows seeing me out here."

We moved inside and went at it in the backseat like we hadn't had sex in years. He was just about to satisfy my desires despite me just being with my fiancé until I saw my self in my rearview mirror. What am I doing? I have a chance at life and I'm getting ready to mess it up for a fuck in the back seat of a car! Just a few months back I was dirty old Parade Knight. Now I'm sexy ass Parade! I don't want to lose everything I have. I can't see it. Jay had his chance with me and he ruined it. And as far as I was concerned, anything that we had together was over.

"Jay," I said in between his lips covering mine. "J…J…Jay."

"Yes, baby?" he said softly kissing my face while his

hands found their home on my breasts.

"Stop."

"What?" he continued groping me.

"Stop…please," I told him backing away. "I'm in love and can't do this to Smokes. You gotta go and you gotta go now."

He stopped. Although he was frustrated he looked at me with disappointment and love. "Parade, I'm wrong. I know this ain't even you no more, but I do care about you. And I wasn't tryin' to parkin' lot pimp you either. I just didn't know when I was goin'see you again. I got anxious and start thinkin' wit' my dick. My bad. But one day you're goin' have to face the fact that you care about me too. I just hope it ain't too late."

With that he left the car, and left me alone. I couldn't help but wonder. Were his words true?

Miss Wayne

SIX MONTHS LATER

Listen to this shit. Smokes has this little girl he calls his *play sister* named Sweets hangin' around him and Miss Parade ever since they got together. Anytime a man calls a girl *play* anything I think they're, fuckin' 'em. And nine times out of ten they are.

Any who, this chick follows Miss Parade around everywhere, even when Miss Parade doesn't want her to. I thinks she a little spy bitch cause she does everything Smokes tells her too including picking out Miss Parades outfits. This brings me to my dilemma of the day. How can I move this bitch out of the way to help Miss Parade buy the proper wedding gown? Knowing me, I'm sure I'll think of something.

"Sorry I'm late, honey." I placed my purse down in Miss Parade's private dressing room. She wanted me to meet her here. This place is called *Bells and Diamonds* and it's a full service wedding planning company. They do everything from picking out the panties you'll wear on your precious day to selecting the food you'll eat on your honeymoon. "So what do we have here?" I asked, hugging Miss Parade then looking at the gowns in the room.

"Thanks for coming, Miss Wayne," Miss Parade said, kissing my face and hugging me close. "This is Sweets, Smokes

play sister." She was being cynical because we joked on a regular about this bitch and the little *play-sister* thing.

"Now, Parade…Smokes' *sister* is sufficient enough after all; I've known him for over two years." She continued, as she reached out her hand to shake mine. She was a pretty little light skin chica with fire red hair. She wore it straight down her back. Her ass was huge and her waist was the width of one of my ankles. *Bitch*. I took one look at her and knew he was fucking her or had fucked her in the past. "It's nice to finally meet you, Wayne."

"Darling, please. Wayne was my father. Call me *Miss* Wayne," I advised her. "My father turned over in his grave ten times already."

"Oh I'm sorry," she smiled courteously. "Miss Wayne, I was just telling Parade that this aqua green gown would look lovely for her bride's maids and that this gown right here," she continued, raising one of the others. "would look excellent on her."

I took one look at that piece of shit and my baby's worried eyes and knew she wasn't puttin' that mess on.

"Ummm, what other selections do we have to choose from?" I asked, sitting on a chair in the dressing room crossing my legs. "Cause this design won't look good on Miss Parade."

"Oh but it does," she continued, waving the gawd awful thing in my face. "This is Emilio Pucci."

"I don't give a rat's ass if it's Emilio's Pussy it's not her style!" I saw a slight smile come over Miss Parade's face which only encouraged me to unleash on this bitch even further. "Now why don't you wiggle your little pretty ass down the hall and get someone to bring us some *serious* options."

Sweets grabbed the dressed and angrily moved toward the exit. She tripped on the end of the gown almost bumping her head against the door.

When she was gone I said, "What's up with Miss

Thang?" Miss Parade was laughing so hard she couldn't even answer. "What? What I do?"

"You are a mess! I'm so glad you're here, Miss Wayne."

"Why wouldn't I come?"

"I don't know…after the thing with me and Daffany *and* finding out I'm with Smokes. I just thought you were through with me."

"I'm not going to lie," I told her crossing my legs to the other side. "I don't like the situation, but I love you. And if you need me, I'll always be here for you. You know that."

She gripped me tightly.

"So what's her story?"

"I don't know. But I think she tryin' to set me up. Did you see that shit?" she asked, putting her hands on her hips. Even in her pearl colored slip she looked beautiful. Her hair was pinned up in a cute little ponytail and she had these diamond earrings on that set the place on fire.

"Did I? She tried to label drop like I give a fuck. Ugly is ugly I don't care what designer made it!"

She laughed until the smile was removed from her face.

"I don't think she likes me," she sat down next to me, laying her head on my shoulder. I tapped her knee and noticed she had lost some more weight. "Whatever I like she likes the opposite. It's like she's prying and trying to draw us apart at the same time."

"Put her in her place." I told her. "This is your wedding!"

"I can't. I feel sorry for her." She walked toward the mirror and looked at herself. "Maybe she thinks with me in the picture, Smokes won't have time for her."

"Well he *will* be a married man." I walked over to the mirror and unraveled her ponytail so that it fell on her shoulders.

"I know…but I know how it feels to be alone." She looked at me through the mirror.

I heard her but I couldn't help but notice how beautiful

Miss Parade was. Her skin was clear and she truly looked flawless.

"You're beautiful," I informed her. "Can you finally see it now? You *really* are beautiful, Miss Parade."

"Miss Wayne, please," Parade attempted to walk away but her steps didn't lead her far. "I don't want to hear that right now."

"Miss Parade, do you know who you are now? I mean really know who you are."

There was a long period of silence.

"I don't know! I don't know," she repeated, dropping her head. She sat down on the bench. "I'm just trying to be happy for what I got. A man who wants me. You know?"

Silence.

"Is your mother coming?" I asked, skipping the subject although I truly prayed for the day when she would finally know her self worth.

"No." She looked down in her lap. "She still hates me for escaping her verbal abuse and I'm through trying to talk to her."

"I don't blame you."

"If she met Smokes I know she'd like him though." Her eyes widened with hope.

"Speaking of Smokes, have you guys discussed *that* night yet?" I was speaking of the night he hired Cannon to murder Sky.

She looked around to be sure Sweets wasn't coming in the room and said, "I'm afraid to."

"Well I think you should. He made a serious threat to all of us and I'd like to be able to rest knowing he doesn't want my nuts on a platter anymore."

"I'm sure your nuts are safe." She laughed.

"You know what I mean. You guys *need* to talk about that night."

"I'm just joking." She rubbed my hand. "I'll talk about it

with him later."

"You sure?"

"Yeah…I've been thinkin' about it too. He never mentioned anything. I mean, at one point he was gonna kill me, you, Sky and Daffany just to find out who killed his wife. And now *I'm* gonna be his wife."

"Right. You sure you know what you're doin', Miss Parade?" I held her beautiful face in my hands. "Cause this is serious. I mean…you shouldn't ask him if you think he can't take it. It might set him off."

We were in a middle of a conversation when Sweets walked back into the room with two dresses in her hand. One looked like it could be used to wrap a truck in and the other looked like an old bed spread.

"Honey, why don't you like Miss Parade?"

"I do," she said placing the dresses down on the stool. "I'm more on her side than you think I am. So why would you say that?"

"Cause you and I both know you wouldn't be caught dead in either of those dresses. So why bring them to us?"

"I would wear these dresses," Sweets covered her mouth with her hands in disbelief. "I wouldn't do anything to hurt Parade."

"Miss Parade, from here on out, I'm taking over your wedding plans."

"Excuse me?" Sweets said, with her hands on her hips. "Smokes trusted me to handle all of the affairs."

"Honey, the only thing you gonna handle is your ass in a seat. I'm not about to stand by and let you ruin my girl's wedding. I've spoken! You're dismissed!"

Sweets got so pissed with me she ran out the dressing room slamming the door shut.

"You know I'ma hear about this shit when I get home right?" Miss Parade slid her clothes giggling the entire time.

"Yeah well if he gets mad tell him to come see me."

"You serious?"

"Girl, I'm just playin' that man'll kill me dead, honey!"

"That's what I thought." She laughed, slipping on her shoes. "But let me get home before she calls him. I'ma talk to you later." She grabbed her purse.

"Wait…you talk to Miss Daffany yet?" I asked, stopping her from leaving momentarily.

"No and I don't want to." Her face appeared crumbled up.

"It's been six months, Miss Parade. When are yall gonna stop this shit?"

"I don't care! She played me with that Jay shit. She knew I was tryin' to get over him and she gonna turn around and have him meet me at IHOP! I'm sick of her!"

"I know. But, bitch you know you wanted to see that man anyway. I'm tired of him askin' about you every time he sees me. And for real, I can tell in his eyes he's in love with you."

For a second I saw the gleam in her eyes, and then it went away.

"I have to get over him, Miss Wayne. He hurt me bad. You know that. Plus I'm getting' married now. He's too late."

He sighed.

"The only reason I'm bringing any of this up is because I can't find her. I went past her old apartment and somebody else lives there and her mother doesn't know her head from her asshole so she can't tell me nothin'. And I saw somebody driving her car. And when I asked them how they got it, they said she sold it to 'em."

I saw by the look in her eyes she was upset. It was obvious she still cared.

"It's not my problem anymore and neither is she."

"Miss Parade, are you changin' on me, suga? I mean lately you've been so cold. Miss Daffany is family and I know you don't mean that."

"Don't tell me what I mean. You heard her! She said we weren't friends so why should I care about her well being?"

"Why are you so critical? I mean, you got what you wanted right? A husband! Shouldn't you be more positive now? You changin' for the worse!""

"I'm not changin', Miss Wayne. I'm just tired of the bullshit that's all. Now let me get home before this girl calls Smokes. I'll call you later to tell you what happened. Love you." She kissed my cheek.

"Love you too baby." I responded as I watched her walk out the door.

The thing you don't understand is this, money and a man changes everything. Especially if you're not use to havin' neither. Miss Parade has to work a lot of shit out on her own. I just hope she doesn't lose herself in the process. Or her friends.

Daffany

Where am I? I…I don't feel too well. And this place doesn't feel familiar to me. I just need to get high. That's it. Once I'm high I won't care where I am. I smell sweat, piss and something else foul all around me and want to throw up. Lately I've been queasy almost every other day. I figured it was my body adjusting to my new choice of high. Heroin. I made that big step after all.

The place I'm in is dark and when I try to move, I feel bodies all around me.

"You up, sexy?" some man called from behind me. I positioned my body in the direction of his voice.

He flipped on a lamp revealing my surroundings and the first thing I focused on was him. Who was he? He was chocolate and so thin, his bones protruded from his face. On the couch he sat overlooking dismay as if he was Satan and this was hell. Maybe it was.

"You gonna be okay, sweetheart," he promised. "I'm gonna take care of you."

His deep base voice rocked the sleeping dead as they came to wondering where their next high would come from. There was trash all over the floors and five to six other people lying up against the walls next to me. I was in a dope house.

"You got anything?" I asked, rubbing my head and then my arms. I remembered him vaguely. The only problem with heroin was that I sometimes suffered from temporary memory loss. I guess it's the way my body dealt with the drug.

"Naw. Why don't you go out there and shake that pretty thing and get some. We'll leave these lazy bitches here and go somewhere else to hit."

"I need somethin' now," I told him not able to whore around without it.

"You dirty, bastard!" a female yelled from the floor in the kitchen. "I found her and you tryna take her from me. She ain't just workin' for you she workin' for us! If it won't for me she'd still be sleepin' behind the Popeye's Chicken."

I remember now. I met that girl when I was tryna find something to eat two weeks ago. I lost my apartment so I had nowhere else to go. Everything in the world I own is gone. I smoked up the four hundred dollars I made from selling the TV and everything else I had last week. I don't even have enough money to call my friends. And when I do get some money, I probably won't call anyway because nothin' means more to me right now than gettin' high.

"I don't belong to nobody!" I told them trying to get up. When I finally made it up, I tried to move comfortably in the shoes I was wearing that were obviously too big for my feet. I felt hands touching my legs as if they were trying to pull me back down. Kicking them off, I moved toward the part of the floor no one was. "Now I'm gonna get some money to buy some more dope but if ya'll want to hit, ya'll gotta help. Hell, this ain't no free world!"

"That's right!" he agreed. "This ain't no free world. And if you don't bring back some of that money you earn, you'll have to find some place else to live. Cause Carmen already told me your homeless. You need me just as much as I need you."

Did he say live? I didn't even know I lived here. I weighed my options quickly in my head and realized I didn't have many. If I reached out to Miss Wayne, he would ask a bunch of questions about my new addiction. And I wouldn't call that

bitch Parade if my life depended on it.

I asked myself over and over why did I go back to Ty that night to cop heroin. I had 100 dollars that Jay gave me and could've spent it anywhere else. Instead I spent it with him. All I remember after smoking was feeling as if I was floating. It was as if nothing else mattered. It was everything he said it would be and more. I experienced orgasms that moved from my head to my toes and held on to me tighter than any man ever could. I was in love. With a drug.

"I'm with you," Carmen said. "So what you waitin' on?" she asked appearing from the shadows. Now that I came down from my high I understand why I trusted her. She reminded me of Sky. She had the same light skin, pretty eyes and soft curly hair. The only difference was that Sky wouldn't be caught dead in a crack house or wearing the same clothes for two days in a row let alone a month.

"I'm startin' to feel sick." I told them rubbing my arms. "So whatever we do we have to do now."

This drug took a lot of my energy. A lot out of me. It required that I catered to it every second of the day. The only time I was free was when I was smoking. So smoking was the only way to feel some relief.

"Me too so let's go." She opened the door.

"You, bitches betta make sure you remember where home is. Both of yall were homeless before I let you in." *I know for a fact I'm not coming back here*. I thought. "You heard me?" he yelled.

"I heard you," I responded not even knowing his name.

"Shut the hell up! We comin' back," she slammed the door behind us.

When we left, Carmen was right on my ass. Now that we were outside I could tell I was off of Minnesota Avenue in D.C.

I was familiar with where I was so finding a trick should be easy. When I spotted a brick building I ran behind it to fix myself up.

"What you doin?"

"Gettin' myself together. Just cause we smoke dope don't mean we got to look like it!"

"I can tell you ain't been in the streets long." She laughed, watching me take off my jeans and shoes. She was looking around to see if anybody was watching us.

"Why you say that?" I asked right before I sniffed my panties and threw them down on the ground. They stunk so bad they made me nauseous. Once they were off I put my jeans back on, and tied a knot in the back of my shirt. It was October and there was a slight nip outside but not too cold to bare.

"Cause these mothafuckas care about one thing and one thing only. Pussy. So all the getting neat shit you doin' is a waste of time." She continued eyeing my stomach. She was a hater and I knew it. "What you need to do is lay off that beer cause yo stomach damn near pokin' out of your jeans." She laughed, pointing her finger at me.

Yeah…this bitch definitely reminds me of Sky. She's so negative she probably doesn't realize she's doing it.

I placed my hands on my hips and said, "Well since you got so much mouth, let's see who can get the most money." I told her as I took out my hair and neatly placed it in a ponytail. My mixed heritage allowed my hair to tame a little better.

"You on," she smirked.

We strolled up and down East Capitol street like D.C.'s finest. Standing in front of the Shrimp Boat, and old restaurant, I knew it was just a matter of time before I made that bitch eat her words. She was on the other end of the boat tryin' to do her thing too. See, she may have been a user longer than me, but I was a whore longer than her and I knew the streets well. I knew what men wanted without even asking. I just hoped smoking didn't throw me off.

“You tryna have some fun, baby?” I asked a car with two boys who didn’t look much older than 17. They motioned to get my attention the moment I gave them eye contact. It was a late model Acura TL so I knew they had a little cash to feed my need.

“I don’t know, let me see your titties first,” the passenger with the Red Sox baseball cap said. His long eyelashes made him look innocent but I’m sure he was far from it.

“That’s gonna cost you more, baby.” I advised lickin’ my lips before puckering them seductively.

“Oh we got dough,” the driver with the corn rolls responded, flashing a knot so big it made my mouth water. There in the middle of the street I lifted my shirt so that he could see my breasts.

“You’re a dirty, bitch!” a woman yelled from another car.

I laughed at her. She calling me a bitch and got a kid with her. Whatever!

“Aight, meet us down that street behind that white house. In the backyard.” He pointed. “My man lives over there.”

“Cool can my friend come too?” I asked pointing at Carmen who was walking back and forth looking dumb. She was no match for me and I knew it. At least I could do was show her how to get cash quick.

They both glanced at her and said, “Oh hell yeah!”

“Cool, why can’t ya’ll just give us a ride right now and then we can do it in the car,” I responded anxiously. As badly as I was feeling, I couldn’t risk them going down the street and not coming back.

“Cause we don’t let whores in our car that’s why,” the driver said angrily.

I rubbed my arms and shook my head. “Okay, we on our way over there.”

They pulled off without further explanation.

When they left I told her everything and she was down for it too. The only thing that got on my nerves was that she kept

asking me a bunch of questions.

"How much money they have?" she looked at me like a kid hopeful she'd get what she wanted on Christmas day.

"Enough."

"How old were they?"

"Does it matter?"

"Do they know I'm coming?" she persisted.

What the fuck was wrong with this bitch? Money was money and all of the questions were irritating and unnecessary at best. So I ignored her and we walked toward the house.

We were at the place he said he'd be for fifteen minutes before they showed up.

"Dats them?" she asked when they arrived. She looked like it was a problem. "They look like kids."

"Well dem kids got money so if you don't want to do it, get the fuck from over here because you ain't bout to fuck my shit up!"

"And let you win the bet?" she rolled her neck and folded her arms. "I'm standing right here."

"Bitch, I already won the bet," I advised her. "Who got they trick asses over here?" I paused. "Me!"

They jumped out of the car and moved toward us. Not only did they look real young, they looked like they were in middle school. Suddenly I was starting to feel some kind of way.

"How old are ya'll?" I asked the one who was driving the car. Both of them looked fresh and I could tell they were drug dealers.

"Well let me see, I'm one hundred dollars, my man right here is one hundred fifty."

"They sound old enough to me," Carmen smiled, dropping to her knees on the grey dirt, no grass. She was in full dick sucking mode.

"Naw we want pussy." The driver spoke.

She got up and looked at me.

"Fine wit me," she continued looking around. "Dis ya'll house? Cause we ain't got no problem goin' inside."

"Naw…this our boy's house. We gonna fuck ya'll right out here." The passenger said. I could tell they were lying about knowing anybody who lived here, but I needed a hit bad so arguing wasn't an option.

"Where you want it?" I inquired looking around the run down backyard.

He pointed to a rusty ass green picnic table. The paint was peeling revealing the ugly cream color beneath it. I felt my sickness coming on and decided we needed to hurry up. Hopefully they had some dope on 'em that way, we wouldn't have to go far to get high.

"Bend over on the picnic table and spread ya'll asses." The driver said as the passenger laughed. We eyed the bench style table.

Looking at each other briefly, Carmen and I did as we were told. Once our clothes were at our knees, we placed our stomachs on the table, our knees on the seat and spread our asses. We wanted this to be over quickly. It was humiliating.

"Aight don't look at us cause we don't like nobody lookin' at us when we fuckin'," the passenger advised giggling the entire time. I heard the faint sound of a chain rattling and panting.

"Aight," Carmen said looking at me strangely. "Did we bother askin' how much money they given us?" she whispered to me as we waited for the ordeal to be over.

"You heard their names. We gonna get over two hundred dollars. That's more than enough."

I was trying not to put too much pressure on my stomach because for some reason it felt tight and hard.

"Damn, ya'll got some pretty pussies,' the driver said.

"Yeah…look at the shorty who looks Chinese," he said talking about me. "Her pussy look like it's smilin' at me," the passenger responded.

"You mind if we lick it first?" the driver asked.

"Whatever floats your boat just hurry up. We tryna get high." Carmen advised.

"We got you. Spread your ass cheeks further apart." Mine was spread so far it felt like it would split. I hated to think of who would pop up and see us. "Yeah that's good."

When I opened all the way, I felt a hard tongue on my pussy. It was rougher than any tongue I ever felt before. I wasn't trippin' because I wasn't tryin' to cum. I was tryin' to get paid. The panting sound grew louder.

"Keep that pussy open," one of them encouraged. We did.

"Aight! Just do what you gotta do so we can leave."

"Get the other one too," the other said. "Spread your pussy open red bone." She did. "Yeah just like that."

"What the fuck?" Carmen said with wide eyes. "Yo, I don't think they licking our pussies." She looked surprised and scared.

"What you mean?" I asked frowning thinking she was complaining again.

"I think it's a dog or something."

"What?" I asked.

I turned around and saw the head of a dog. I jumped up and almost threw up after seeing that shit. These little mothafuckas had a nerve to be filming us on a camera phone getting eaten out by a big ass German Sheppard. I tried to pull up my jeans but they were so tight it was taking too much time so I ran with them falling at my ankles. Carmen was right behind me but she had hers pants pulled up already. I had one thing and one thing only on my mind, getting that camera. The thing about it was, had they paid us, it probably would not have mattered.

"Give me that camera, bitch!" I screamed.

"I told you this was some bullshit!" Carmen called out adding to my fury.

I felt like a fool. I was running down the block with my ass out no panties. When I finally got my pants up I ran smack dab into a police car. I turned around to see where Carmen was and noticed she was gone. That dirty bitch must've seen them coming and didn't warn me.

The officer jumped out of the car and instructed me to put my hands on top of it. "Put your fuckin' hands on the car!" the black male officer screamed.

"What's the charge?" I asked already knowing the answer.

"Indecent exposure," he advised. Moving in closer he really let me know how he felt when he said, "And for being a dirty fuckin' whore who's pregnant!"

And that's how I found out I was carrying a baby.

Shit! Now what?!!!

Parade

Our kitchen always made me relaxed. The royal blue painted walls with yellow highlights on the borders gave it a rustic and quiet appeal. And the stainless steal refrigerator, countertops and cabinets made it look even more powerful. I had prepared dinner and all of the lights were out with the exception of the long candles I lit on the table.

Although everything appeared perfect on the outside, for real it wasn't. I caught Smokes putting something in my toner and I needed to know what it was. The sad part is, I'm afraid to ask.

"How's dinner?" I asked Smokes as we enjoyed our meal. I looked at his handsome face across the candle's glow. I prepared steak, mashed potatoes and garlic green beans.

"It's cool; I got some things to take care of later so I can't eat long." He placed the silver fork in his mouth before reaching for another bite.

"I understand," I said cutting a piece of my steak. "I have a few things to talk to you about, though."

"Like what?"

"Today… I came in the bathroom and saw you putting something in the toner for my face? What was it?"

He dropped the fork and carefully picked it back up. He looked as if I'd caught him in something. But what?

"It's nothing. Just skin bleach."

Skin bleach? I thought.

"I don't understand," I frowned and could feel my blood boiling. "Why would you do that?"

"Because I'm looking out for you that's why," he said with ease. I sensed that he didn't care about how he made me feel. "Anybody on my arm has to look the part. You know that."

"Oh," I whispered. His reason hurt. One minute I was pretty enough and the next minute I wasn't.

"So what's the other thing?"

"Huh?" I asked still confused by his response.

"You said you had to talk to me about a *few* things."

"Oh yeah," I focused on my plate instead of his face.

"Cause I actually want to talk to you about a few things too," he took his final bite before dropping his fork on the plate.

"Did you want to go first?" I questioned wondering what he could possibly want to talk to me about.

"Naw…tell me what else is on ya mind. It's obvious the bleach thing wasn't all you wanted to know. You been kinda short all day."

"Ok," I wiped my mouth with a paper towel. "Baby, this is hard for me but it has been on my mind. Uh…ah…don't know how to begin."

"You want to know if I still plan on killin' you and your friends."

Long silence.

I stared into his eyes wondering how long he had known that I wanted the answer to that question. And most of all why he kept me in suspense so long.

"Yes. That's it." I was unable to look at him.

"I got to give you credit." He laughed. "Talk about unconditional love. You waited until now to ask me about that shit accepting my ring and everything. You pretty, gangsta."

I felt desperate.

"But since I plan on makin' you my wife we might as well get the shit out in the open. But after this, I don't want to talk about it again. Got it?"

"Yes." I smiled weakly.

"Cool," he paused. "when I found out that my wife had been killed at the party ya'll went to, I was fucked up. I couldn't understand how number one somebody could get me wrong by fuckin' with mine," he pointed at himself. "and number two how they could kill somebody who ain't do shit to 'em. First I thought it was drug related. You know…a nigga tryin' to get at me got at her instead. And then I find out that Sky killed her from somebody at the party. And then I remembered meeting her at the movie theater one day earlier that week."

"At the movies?"

"Yeah…her and that nigga *Jay*," he placed emphasis on his name. "came up there when we were catchin' a flick," Smokes folded his arms revealing his sparkling diamond Rolex Presidential watch. "This bitch Sky was doin' everything in the world to get my attention. She was giving me the eye while her nigga was buying snacks and bending down in front of my dick. She was on it hard. So I knew she was sweatin' me. And I ain't gonna lie; I woulda smashed her if sheda waited. So when she was killed," he breathed heavily.

I started putting everything together. Ida neva thought she would go as far. I mean…she was on some whole notha shit to take my wife's life. I knew you, Daffany and that faggy ain't have shit to do with it, but I didn't want the heat brought to me from ya'll snitchin'. So I sent Cannon to be sure. And you know the rest," he ate some more of his meal. "But when I met you, I didn't even know who you were. Back in the day when I use to see you, you were fightin' and playin' in the streets. I was surprised to see you come up and I couldn't believe how good you looked. So I had to check you, to see what you were like."

"It didn't bother you that I got with Cannon?"

"Naw. It didn't."

I didn't believe him.

"Trust me, I ain't trip off of none of that shit," he said as if he'd been reading my mind. "If I plan on wifin' you that means I trust you. And I trust you now."

I smiled.

"But I do want you to be real wit me," he said seriously. "Are you fuckin' that kid Jay?"

"What you talkin' 'bout?" I asked as I almost choked on my steak.

"Parade, don't play me. Remember I said I trust you, don't fuck that up." He said pointing the tip of his fork at me.

"No I'm not," I replied as my hand unconsciously shook against my plate. I wondered if someone saw us in front of the IHOP acting like freaks.

"You sure?" he said eyeing my hand.

I moved it. "Yes…I'm positive."

"Cause I'm hearin' things I don't like to hear around the way," he told me. "And you know I still run the Manor."

"I know. But have you been hearin' things recently?"

"No."

"Cuz I promise you its over between us. It was over a long time ago."

"Good, you still want to be with me?"

I waited to answer the question. My soul didn't feel completely safe with Smokes anymore yet I became accustomed to the lifestyle I was living.

"Yes…I still want to be with you."

"Good, cause we have something else to talk about. I might need you real soon. Really, really soon and I need to know I can count on you."

Smokes had been saying that a lot and whenever I asked him what he needed me to do, he'd never answer.

"Well what is it? You know I'd do anything for you."

"We'll talk about it later," he told me. "On some other shit, Sweets told me you let *Mr. Chokes-on-dick* interfere wit' our business."

"Not really. It's just that I think some of that shit she was pickin' out, she was tryin' to set me up."

He laughed and stroked his goatee. "Parade, you new money, baby. Don't act like you know everything there is about living the life. You still got a lot of work to do before you start venturing off on your own. Now let Carmen help plan the wedding. And keep ya friends out of my business. There might come a time when you'll have to cut them off altogether, anyway. They're not in your league anymore."

"But they're my friends.

"You heard me right?"

I nodded.

"Aight? That's my, girl." He said softly. "The bleach is working too. Your complexion is clearing up."

"Thanks." I nodded.

"Now finish your meal," he winked. "But don't eat too much. We gotta watch that figure."

"Can you meet me at sixth district?" Miss Wayne yelled in my cell phone. I switched to my Bluetooth so I could have my hands free.

"What for?" I asked in between washing the dishes. Smokes didn't like them in the dishwasher so I cared for them by hand. I'll be so happy when the maid comes back from vacation because this house is too big for me to clean on my own.

"Miss Daffany is in jail."

"So?! She stays in and out of jail."

"But she's pregnant too," he told me. "*Now* can you meet me?"

I dropped a plate, grabbed my purse and ran out the door.

"Hey, pretty!" Miss Wayne said wearing a one piece white Lycra dress and white high heels. He let his hair grow out long enough to wear tracks. He kept his hair in what he called the *Beyonce*, which consisted of a goldish long flowing weave. "Can you believe this shit?"

"No what she do?" I asked, as we sat down in the seats waiting on her to appear. Miss Wayne had already paid her bail.

"They said some indecent exposure shit. I'm just happy to find her. I can't believe it took all this?" he said reaching for my hand. I gave it to him and squeezed his lovingly.

"How did you find out she's pregnant?"

"She told me. I guess she didn't believe I'd come without telling me. But you know I been tryin' to find this chile for months now. I'm worried about her, Miss Parade. They say she fuckin' wit heroin now."

"Heroin?" I yelled looking into his eyes. "Are you serious?"

"Yes! Between my mother and you guys, I don't have any other family. I can't see losing somebody else. Sky was enough, Miss Parade," he said, squeezing my hand almost tighter than I could stand. "We have to keep what's left of us together and you and Miss Daffany are gonna have to bury this beef."

"Yeah…maybe we can get pass this *if* she can accept my husband." I sighed. "I doubt she'll be able to though. She's made that clear."

"Yeah well one step at a time." He laughed. "The first thing is repairing *our* bond and *our* family."

Just then I stared at the door and could've sworn I saw a ghost. This dusty girl came rushing into the police station and she looked so much like Sky, it was eerie. Miss Wayne must've thought so too because he looked at her and than back at me.

"Doesn't she look like-,"

"Sky?" I finished.

"Hell yeah!"

Just then Daffany came out. We stood up and stared at the unsightly mess before us. She looked so terrible I was about to cry. She was completely skinny with the exception of her protruding stomach. We went to greet her but she walked directly to the Sky look-a-like.

"Miss Daffany," Miss Wayne said tears in his eyes as he walked behind her. "What has happened to you?"

We walked over to them.

"What you talkin' 'bout?" she asked, tugging on her dirty t-shirt as if straightening it would make her look better. "I'm fine." The girl remained by her side looking us up and down. "And what the fuck is she doin' here?" Daffany asked pointing at me.

"I came to see about you." I told her, angry she tried to get out on me. I couldn't even argue because I was consumed with pity. "What is going on with you, Daffany? Look at you? Are you even eating?"

"Bitch, please! You don't care about nobody but yourself! I don't want to see you ever again and I mean it!" she yelled at me before focusing on Miss Wayne. "Miss Wayne, can you give me some money please? I have a job that starts tomorrow and I'll pay you back everything. I just need some money for the bus."

"You do?" her friend asked looking confused. "When you get an interview?"

"Yo, shut the fuck up!" she screamed. "You betta be glad I don't jump in your shit for leaving me hanging. I know you saw the cops comin'," she continued before addressing Miss Wayne again. "Do you got it or not?"

"You know I do, Miss Daffany, but won't you come with me. I want to help you. Let me take care of you."

"I don't need any help." She told him rubbing her arms. "I just need some money to go to work tomorrow. I'll pay you back plus the money for bail."

"Daffany, won't you just go with him? Nobody came out

here to give you no money for you to get back on the streets!" I yelled. "Don't be as stupid as you look!"

"Why don't you mind your business?!" the girl said to me.

"Uh...honey...don't get fucked up." Miss Wayne told her. "Trust me. I'm saving your life and your narrow ass."

"Please, Miss Wayne." Daffany said, interrupting his attention off the bitch. "I need you. Please help me. *Pleeeeaaasse*."

Miss Wayne looked at her, and then at me. I turned away. He and I both knew what she wanted the money for. So if he wanted to give it to her I wanted no part of it. He reached in his purse and handed her a wad of cash. Before he released it into her grip he said, "If you need me you can call me. I'm serious, baby. No matter what you're going through, you have to know that I will *ALWAYS* be there for you."

"I know," she said hugging him. "I'll pay you back every penny you'll see!"

"It's fine. Don't worry about it." He said rubbing his hand over her belly. "You know it's not too late for the baby? The baby can be born healthy without the dis-."

"Don't say that!" Daffany yelled, looking at Carmen. I knew then that she didn't tell her she was infected because she stopped Miss Wayne before he could say *disease*. "Just let me live my life." With that she was gone with the bitch out the door.

Miss Wayne broke out in tears. I never seen him cry like that in all my years of knowing him. I was hurt because he was hurt. I love Miss Wayne like a brother, but stronger. This shit was not fair to him and he did not deserve it!

"Miss Wayne...you got to pull yourself together." I told him rubbing his back. "We can't help her if she doesn't want it."

"But I'm worried, Parade." He must've been devastated because he didn't say *Miss* before my name and that pissed me off even more. He always took care of me so I decided to look

after him for a change even if he didn't want me to. "Give me a sec." I ran toward the door.

"Where you goin?" he called out.

"I'll be back."

I ran out the door and caught up to them quick. It wasn't hard considering they were on foot.

"Daffany!" I yelled. They both turned around.

"What do you want?" Daffany said pausing for me.

When I got up on her, I smacked the living shit out of her.

Her *fiend*, I mean *friend* stepped like she was going to make a move.

"Try it, bitch and I'll stomp you back to the first day you fucked your life up!" I promised pointing my finger in her face.

She remained still but crossed her arms over her chest.

"Now let me tell you something, Daffany. You can be mad at me all you want. As a matter of fact, I understand your hate towards me, but that man back there loves you. You walked all over his heart and left me to pick up the pieces and I hate you for it. If you want to smoke that shit up its fine by me. In fact," I paused reaching in my purse dropping over four hundred dollars in cash on the ground. "Take mine too, but don't call him no more! Let him get over this shit cause you and I both know you ain't gonna change. And I promise, if I find out you're using him, I'll kill you! And I mean it!"

She bent down picked up the money and wiped a tear from her face.

"Damn, I guess you finally know who you are," she said looking at the drug money my husband earned in her hands. "Like husband like wife. Don't worry, I'll stay out of his life, and yours too. Consider me as dead as Sky. That should make it easy for you."

"Come on. We can still catch Tyrone if we hurry!" Carmen said uncaring about how Daffany felt at the moment. "Let me hold the money."

"Bitch, please I got this!" she told her.

She took one last look at me and walked hand and hand with Carmen until they were totally out of sight.

And I wondered, what happened to my friend. But most of all, I wondered what happened to me.

Smokes

Smokes was driving in his white Hummer on the way to get it washed at Laurel Car Wash off of Baltimore avenue in Maryland. In his mind, no one knew how to clean his truck better than the Mexican employees who worked there. He was getting ready to open his third beer knowing full well he was a target for the cops by driving a white truck with illegally tinted windows. But opening the beer and pouring it to his lips while bumping loud ass music was a testament of his lack of respect for the law.

His phone rang and he was upset because he was just getting into his favorite song off of Jeeze's CD called "Hypnotize". Whoever it was, he wanted them to be quick.

"Speak on it."

"Smokes, its Silver. You got a sec?"

This bitch nigga is gettin' on my fuckin' nerves. He thought.

"What's good?"

"When we gonna take care of that thing?"

"What thing?" Smokes asked as he pulled into the car wash's parking lot. There was a long line so he knew it would be about thirty minutes before they even looked at his truck. He had plenty of time to discuss the matter with Silver. Instead he said, "Hurry up! I'm busy."

"Well dis nigga runnin' around here like he's untouchable! I'm tired of seein' 'em. Every time I look at this Debarge

lookin' faggot I feel like crackin' his fuckin' skull."

Silver was talking about Jay. Ever since Jay put a hit on his brother Markee while he was in jail which resulted in his murder, he had been heated. Silver didn't care that his lil brother had raped and robbed Jay's cousin. None of that mattered to him.

"I feel you, but didn't I say shit is too hot for me?"

Silver let out a heavy sigh.

"Yeah but he was my brother."

"I know who he was, but Markee got dealt with because he raped that nigga's cousin. What's done is done."

Silence

"So it's like that?" Silver barked.

"It's just like that," Silver yelled back. "Plus I'ma need his ass later. You gonna have to just chill."

"But this shit is fucked…"

Silence.

"DID YOU FUCKIN' HEAR ME?" Smokes yelled causing Silver's heart to pump fear instead of blood.

"Yeah." He said trying to be cool even though he was about to piss his pants. There was no denying he was frightened when it came to Smokes.

He could hear Silver breathin' hard from frustration and decided to fuck with him a little. And although he didn't like Jay because he knew he could get in Parade's head and turn things around, he had to be easy. He him needed him alive for his own purposes.

"What you poutin' for?"

"I ain't poutin'." Silver lied.

"Well you sound like you poutin' like a l'il bitch over there." He said in an authoritative tone. "Now tell me you understand and agree with me."

"What?" Silver said with a little buck in his voice.

"I said tell me you understand, and that you agree with everything I say because I know better than you."

Silver was silent and Smokes decided to put the fire under him.

"Are you hearin' me? Or do I have to make a visit for you to feel me instead?"

Silver breathed heavily and submitted.

"I understand…and…agree with everything you say because you know better than me." He recited like a mad 10 year old little girl.

"Now get out there and make my money."

With that he hit the end call button on his Apple Iphone and smiled.

"Anotha nigga in check."

He was about to be next in line to get his car washed until the phone rang again. This time the caller's number was unknown but he knew exactly who it was, Ace.

"Speak on it."

"What's up with the girl?" the caller asked with a heavy Dominican accent.

"Everything's going as planned."

"Everything's going like whose plans? Yours or mine?"

"Ours."

"Listen you black, nigger," Ace said disrespecting his heritage. "I want you to do whatever you have to quickly! You fucked up the last time and we won't have that problem again. That 'lil bitch will make me a lot of money and I want her as planned. Do I make myself clear?"

"Yeah."

"And she better look like you says she does."

"She does."

"Good. Now get her here!"

The caller hung up. Smokes felt punked and if Silver would've heard the call he would've called it poetic justice. Smokes was furious.

He was so angry that the moment he opened the door to

allow the Mexican driver to take his truck to be cleaned, he stole him in the face. The small man dropped to the ground gripping his mouth while people looked on in disgust. He needed to take his anger out on someone and didn't stop to think about who would take the brunt of his hate.

Now realizing his error, he helped the man off the ground and shoved three hundred dollars in his hand for the trouble. The man wiped the blood from the corner of his mouth and looked at him in horror.

Handing him the keys he said, "Don't forget the tires."

Miss Wayne

"Excuse me have you seen her?" I asked a few people around East Capitol street in D.C. I heard that Miss Daffany stayed in a dope house somewhere in this area and was determined to find her tonight. As I showed the picture of her before she got on heroin, I hoped someone would recognize her even though she didn't look the same.

"Why don't you get in the car, baby?" Dayshawn asked. He was a gay friend of mine that I'd been hanging with recently. I've known him for a long time but wasn't as close with him as I was with Miss Parade and Miss Daffany. He was what I considered a quiet Gay. His style was preppy like Kanye West and he wore a lot of pastel colors. He was certainly fly. Like right now he had on a dark pink polo vest a white button down shirt and light blue jeans. Ever since Parade didn't want to hear anything about Daffany, he was the only one I talked to. "It's getting dark out here and we been outside all day." He continued, following me slowly in the car as I walked up the street.

"I can't leave until I find her. You know that!" I screamed. I was wearing sneakers, sweat pants and a baggy sweat shirt. Outside of my hair in a ponytail, it was the closest I came to looking like a boy in years. "I have to bring her home tonight!" Tears ran down my face. "If you can't understand that you can just leave!"

"You know I'm not gonna do that, baby. Just do what you must." He said, as he continued to follow me.

When my phone rang I anxiously answered it without looking at the number. I got a new cell phone and put the number on my voicemail at home for Miss Daffany to reach me in case she called.

"Hello. Miss Daffany, is this you?"

"No, Miss Wayne it's Parade. Where are you?"

"I'm out." I sighed.

"Out where?" she persisted. "I've been trying to reach you for weeks."

I had been deliberately ignoring her because lately all I could think about was Miss Daffany and that unborn baby she was carrying. And since Miss Parade didn't want to talk about her, I left her alone. It had been a few months since we saw Miss Daffany at the police station and I was worried sick.

"I've been looking for Miss Daffany."

She sighed.

"What's wrong with you?" she screamed into the phone. "The girl doesn't want to be found can't you understand that?! Why are you doing this to yourself? It's ridiculous!"

"I know, Miss Parade but I can't help it. I have to try! She ain't got nobody out here but me since you turned your back on her too."

"Miss Wayne, that girl is gone! Nobody can help her now. Trust me, she's not the same person we use to know."

"I don't want to believe that." I told her getting into the passenger seat of Dayshawn's black Acura. Dayshawn parked and let me talk to her knowing when I was done, I'd be right back out there looking for my friend. "All she needs is love. If you were sick wouldn't you want somebody to be there for you?"

Silence.

"You care about her more than me!"

"What?" I asked not sure if I heard her correctly.

"I said you care about her more than me!"

"That's not fair!"

"Well that's how it seems!" she cried. "I'm getting married and you not even here for me. You steady runnin' around town tryin' to find Daffany's-fuckin'-fiend ass! What about me? Huh?"

"Parade, please," I shook my head and looked up. "That girl is alone out here!"

"Oh so now I'm Parade!" she sobbed. "I ain't got nobody either! Remember that while you outside at night chasin' zombies!"

When she ended the call I fell back in my car seat. I can't believe this chile is doing this to me right now. Mentally I can't deal! She know I love her more than anything but I love Miss Daffany too. I think she's taking her problems out on me because although she's getting married, she's not happy. I was so pissed I *almost* didn't even feel like looking for Miss Daffany anymore. I was done.

"Excuse me? Ya'll lookin' for Daffany the Dopehead?" a little boy said approaching my car window.

I looked at Dayshawn and back at him. Did God answer my prayers so soon? It hurt to hear the name he gave her but I was relieved he knew who she was.

"Yes, honey?" I looked him over. He had to be about twelve years old. "You know where she is?"

"Yeah…she be at the Smokehouse. It's around da corner. I can take you dere for some money."

"Uh…sure, honey." I reached into my purse. "Take it! Just get in and show us the way."

"You sure about this?" Dayshawn asked unlocking the door for the kid to get in.

"What you think?" I responded.

He sighed and pulled off. After a few minutes of driving we arrived at a large group of houses. They looked run down and dilapidated.

"Dere the house right there?" He pointed to the worst

looking one of all. It was green and most of the windows were shattered. “Ya’ll can let me out here.”

“Hey, you don’t want to wait for us to take you home?” I asked, realizing it was too late to have somebody’s child out on the street looking for dope heads.

“I ain’t got no home.” He said, as he jumped out of the car and ran down the street.

We watched him disappear into the night and felt pity. Had I had more time, I would’ve grabbed his little ass and demanded that he let us take him somewhere. But I had neither the time nor the patience.

“Wait right here.” I told Dayshawn preparing to exit the car.

“I don’t like this, baby.” He said grabbing my arm. “Can’t we come back during daytime?”

“No! I might lose her if we wait.” I snatched away from him.

“Please be careful. And if she don’t want to come, don’t force her.” He yelled.

“I’m not leaving out of there without her.” I told him as I unbuckled my seat belt and moved toward the run down house.

When I got behind the old green house I saw a bordered up door. It didn’t appear as if anybody could come in and out of it so, I figured there had to be another way. When I looked down I saw a dark hole with steps leading within it. That’s must be how they got inside.

The smell hit me the moment I took the first step. But my love for Miss Daffany pushed me forward. If Miss Parade was gonna give up on her she’d have to live with it but I wasn’t. The moment my foot hit the last step water splashed inside my tennis shoes causing it to make a squishy noise when I walked. It was disgusting and I hated being wet. I could only pray it was musty old water and not piss. The moment I entered the house somebody reached for me begging for money. I kicked him off and

gripped my arms hoping I'd live long enough to help Miss Daffany out if she was in there. I didn't want any of my limbs hanging. People continued to reach for me like they were in hell and needed an escape. Maybe they were.

When I turned a dark corner I saw a candle on the ground and a dude giving another dude a blow job and even I was disgusted. Walking past them did nothing to stop their rhythm. As I continued down the path I came to a bigger room. The smell was so strong I was sure I smelled it before. It was the day we popped up over my grandmother's house to check on her and she was dead. She had been that way for weeks. I was sure a corpse lied amongst them and either they didn't know or care.

"Do you know Daffany?" I asked a stranger who was lying up against the wall nodding off. There appeared to be thirty or so people in the broken down house. The person ignored me, appearing half dead.

I repeated the same question ten times before I finally spotted her. She was lying on the bare floor her pregnant belly straight up in the air. I gasped seeing her like that. How could she come to this?

She was completely naked and appeared so thin that had it not been for looking for someone pregnant, I would not have known it was her. A man crawled on top of her gripping her legs and pressing her belly without regard for her position. Seeing this, I rushed past everyone to get at her kicking people in the process. This dirty mothafucka had her legs spread a part while he moaned inside of her.

"Get the fuck off of her!" I screamed grabbing him by his neck throwing him to the floor. His monstrous dick was rock hard.

"What the fuck?" he responded, too high to challenge me.

"I will kick your ass if you come near me!" I told him. "Get up, Miss Daffany!" I grabbed her arm as delicate as possible but forceful enough to lead her out. I had plans to take off my

sweatshirt and put it on her naked body the moment we got outside but first, I needed to get her out of that house before these mothafuckas got up and decided to hurt me.

She moved very little and I decided to carry her when I realized walking wasn't working. The stank from her body was atrocious. We were out in the backyard when I gently put her down on the grass. Stooping down I was preparing to take off my sweatshirt until she wrapped her limp arms around me. I held her tightly happy that she recognized me. But instead of speaking, she went tugging at my pants instead.

"What you want your dick sucked?" she said going for my zipper. "I can suck it for you real good if you let me. I just need to get *hiiiiiiiigggh*."

"Miss Daffany, please!" I hit her hands. "It's me! Miss Wayne!"

She stopped reaching for me and wept. She appeared conscious but I could tell she didn't recognize me. And then she smiled and I wondered what brief moments filled her mind to remind her who I was. Was it the times we played on the playground in Elementary school? Or was it the time when me, Miss Sky, Miss Parade and her ran away from home just to be together after a party.

"Ooooohhh, MissWayne," she replied her eyes half closed. "You like it kinky huh? I'll call you whatever you like"

Didn't she know who I was? Did the drug have her mind that gone? I could barely see her face because tears flooded my eyes so I pushed her hands off.

"Miss Daffany, please! I'm family!"

I was somehow able to get my sweatshirt off and onto her when I felt a blow against the back of my head. The pain was blinding. I fell face first on the grass and received another blow to the back of my head. It felt like rocks were in my mouth due to my tooth being cracked. Finally able to turn around, I placed my arms out in front of me to stop any more blows. One by one they hit me with a bat, back to back. All I could see was their feet. One of them had on some old white Air Force Ones and the other had on some run over yellow Timberland boots.

"Help!!!! Please!" I screamed hoping Dayshawn would hear me. "What did I do to you?!"

They didn't answer. Just kept hitting and kicking me.

I looked up and saw Daffany scoot back away from me on the grass. She looked nervous and scared. And although her breasts were covered with my shirt, her vagina was exposed. There was so much blood on my face that it was useless trying to identify the suspects now. The more they hit me, the more I didn't feel the blows. I knew I'd be dead if they continued.

"Get the, bitch!" one of them yelled. "And hurry up before she gets away!"

I guess Miss Daffany was about to run when they directed their attention to her. I was thinking about my next move until I heard…*click.* It sounded like a gun and I knew I would die. My mother would not be able to take me being murdered. What about Miss Parade? She couldn't survive without me either. Why hadn't I listened to them? I was so stupid.

And then I heard, "Unless you want a bigger whole in the tip of your dick then the one God blessed you with, I suggest you put her down and get the fuck out of here."

It was Dayshawn!

"We ain't got no business with you!" a man's voice said. "We just want the girl. She makes us a lot of money."

"Did you hear me? Cause the next thing I say will hurt I promise you."

"Fuck her!" the other man said. "She ain't worth it! We can get another whore way better than her someplace else. And one who looks better."

I heard them run and then I heard Dayshawn's footsteps rush over toward me.

"Look at you!" he said touching my face. "Oh my gawd!

Are you okay, honey?" he said lifting my head sniffling.

"Yes! Is Miss Daffany okay?"

"She's right here. Let me get you to the car and I'll come back for her."

"No…please, take her first!" I told him. My head hurt so bad it was terrible.

"Miss Wayne, I'm not leaving you!"

"And I'm not leaving without her! Now take her first. Please, Dayshawn," I pleaded with him. "Cause if I leave her, and she gets away, all of this will be for nothing."

Silence.

"Bitch, you gonna cause my ulcer to flare up!' he said to me as I heard him stand up. "I'll be right back."

I heard him grunt like he was lifting her up and I was relieved. Everything in me just wanted Miss Daffany to be okay. And it all most cost me my life.

Parade

It was a beautiful day for a concert. And as I sat outside of Miss Wayne's apartment complex waiting on him to come out, I admired the peacefulness while I could. That would all change the moment Miss Wayne stepped foot in this car and found out who I had with me. He's gonna kill me! But trust me, it was beyond my control. I brought Sweets to prevent an argument with Smokes and now I was gonna start one with Miss Wayne, instead. I was starting to wonder if it would be worth it.

"Where you at?" I called his house phone. I'd been sitting outside of the apartment he shared with his lover for over twenty minutes. And we had forty minutes to make it to the concert and it wasn't lookin' good! He told me he was coming downstairs a long time ago! "We gonna be late for the concert! Shit! I want to see the opening act too."

"Calm down, Miss Parade! I tell you, I'll be glad when this wedding thing is over because you've been a royal bitch lately."

"That's your opinion," I told him frowning at his comment. "But I spent $90.00 for these tickets each *and* I'm picking you up. The least you could do is be on time. You told me you liked Corrine Bailey."

"And I do!" he said sounding out of breath.

"I can't tell cause it seems like I spent this money for nothin'."

"And I never done nothin' for you? Hold on, Miss Parade." He said cutting me off. "Miss Daffany, can you take the potato salad out of the fridge and put it in the picnic bag by the door please? Thank you, baby."

I hated that she still lived with him. He was hardly available for me. Back in the day if I called him he was always there. Now I could be dead for all he knew and he could probably care less. And I was sure he was still having problems with Daffany using dope, even though he'd never admit it to me. There's no way a dope head can all of a sudden stop based on sheer determination alone. I for one wasn't buying it.

"And while you're running your mouth, you could be up here helping me with these bags."

"Bags?" I had purchased our seats on the lawn of the outdoor venue and you were allowed to bring outside food. But why was he bringing *bags*? To me one was enough.

"Yes bags! Now hurry up here before we're *really* late."

"I'm not tryin' to be bothered with that zombie?" I adjusted the rearview mirror so that it faced me. "Where is *the dope head* anyway? I'm not trying to see her."

"Where you think she at? Didn't you just hear me talk to her?"

"Yeah whatever," I sighed. "And what about your man? He can't help you bring the bags downstairs?"

"He's out of town and don't flatter yourself about Miss Daffany! This chile ain't hardly thinkin' about you."

"Shoot!" I yelled, turning the mirror back in its correct position so that it focused on the road behind me. Let me hurry up so I can get this over with cause going back and forth with him is a losing battle. "I'm on my way up!"

Miss Wayne's place was always so cozy. Dark burgundy was dominant for his color scheme. It blended well with the green curtains he chose and the dark blue sofa. He knew how to make you feel at home when you stepped through his door.

Everything was neat and the house smelled of the banana bread candles he purchased from *Bed Bath and Beyond.*

He opened up the door without saying anything when I knocked and continued about his apartment like I wasn't even there. I saw three picnic bags already by the door and wondered how many people he thought he was feeding tonight. This was enough food to feed a small village.

"*All* this goin' with us?" My statement caused him to break his busy body motion for one moment. I picked up one bag and noticed it was heavy.

"Yeah." He placed saran wrap over a bowl of fried chicken. "I got one more bag and then we good to go."

I loved this man all my life. And don't get it twisted, I appreciate everything he does for me, but he's getting on my last fuckin' nerves! He was the reason I could hardly lose weight. He cooks for every occasion. Somebody's birthday…he's cooking. A holiday…he's cooking. Somebody's taking a shit…he's cooking. It's ridiculous!

"Hey, Parade." Daffany spoke appearing from the back room. Her stomach was extra large and she was real skinny. She looked bad. *Real bad.* I felt my nose stinging. It was the sensation I got whenever I was on the verge of crying. How could she let herself fall like this and force me and Miss Wayne to watch her? I hated her for the pain she was causing me. And I hated her for the pain she was causing *us*.

"Daffany." I said dryly not in the mood for a conversation with that bitch. My eyes roamed everywhere but on her. "Well I'm bout to take this stuff outside, Miss Wayne." I grabbed two of the picnic bags and threw them over one arm and held the third in my hand. "I'll be waitin' for you in the car."

"Hold up I'm comin' now!" he said grabbing his oversized Marilyn Monroe meets Car Windshield shades. "Honey, you gonna be okay?" he asked Daffany swinging his white leather purse over his shoulder. He had on blue velour pants, and

a matching blue velour top with blue strap sandals. His toes were damn near hanging over the edge.

"Yes! Go ahead!" she smiled. I could see she was uncomfortable because she looked at me then back at him. It must be hard being treated like a kid. But this is all her fault. "I have the food you made me in the microwave and I'm gonna sit here and watch *Stomp The Yard* for the fiftieth time today." She continued laughing touching her belly.

"If you need me, call me on my cell phone. I have it with me." He said touching his bag before bending down to kiss her swollen belly. "And if you have to run out anywhere, take your key."

You mean this bitch has a key? I thought.

Why's he giving her so much attention? Its cause of her he has a big gash across his forehead from the day he found her wretched ass at the dope house. And if it wasn't for the tracks he wore you'd be able to see he had stitches in the back of his head too.

"Miss Wayne, we gonna be late!" I reminded him opening the front door jingling my car keys for emphasis. "Daffany's a grown ass woman!"

This was his cue to come on! I felt consumed with jealousy and I didn't know why. I have to get out of here.

He shot me the evil eye and kissed Daffany one last time before walking out the door with me. I couldn't help but wonder if I was still his favorite. I was the one he always rescued in our little group. I don't want things to change. Too much has changed already in my life. Sky's dead. Daffany's on heroin and I might be losing Miss Wayne's love. He was the only person consistent in my life, and I needed to know he would always be there for me…regardless.

When he saw Sweets sitting in my car I knew he was gonna unleash. And unleash is what he did. It wasn't my fault. Smokes insisted that I bring her along, and she gladly obliged.

She loved spying on me. She and I both knew it. It was almost as if she was trying to catch me in something. But what?

"Is there a problem?" she asked glaring at him, as she roamed through the hair magazine I picked up earlier from the grocery store.

I wanted to change my hair for my wedding so we were going over different styles. I had settled on letting my natural hair fall in a medium length bob. Miss Wayne stood outside the car shooting daggers at her.

"Yes there's a problem." He pulled down his shades so that they rested on the tip of his nose, allowing him to peer over them. "For one you're here, and for two you're in the front seat. So why don't you wiggle your little narrow azz in the back where you belong."

"What?!" she slammed the magazine shut, throwing it in her lap. "You didn't *call* front seat!"

"I didn't *call* front seat? Chile…you're about to get what I call an old fashioned ass kicking if you don't slither in the back! Ya heard?"

She looked at me and all I could say was, "Just slither in the back seat before he gets angry."

She huffed and puffed the entire time but she moved where she belonged. The magazine dropped on the floor of my car and she didn't bother picking it up. Messing with a faggy was out of the question and I did her a favor by making her go where it was harder for him to slap her. When she put her seat belt on, he threw the picnic bags over her tossing the magazine in her face.

"Ouch!" she exclaimed rubbing her cheek.

"Shut up, huzzy!" He got in the front placing his seat belt on next.

Boy am I gonna hear about this shit from Smokes later.

"Why is she here?" He turned up the music as if she was a child and couldn't hear over the sounds blaring from the speak-

ers.

"Cause he wanted her here." I pulled out of the parking lot of his apartment complex in Bowie. It would take us 45 minutes to drive to Columbia Maryland's Merriweather Post Pavilion, an outside concert hall.

"Well why would he want her here when he knows I can't stand her yella ass?!"

"Miss Wayne, please!" I looked at him before focusing back on the road. "You're yella too. Or have you forgotten?"

"Miss Parade, is that man beating you?" he continued drilling me like a sergeant.

"What?" I glared at him as I merged into traffic. "What are you talkin' about now?"

"I said is he beating you?"

"No he's not beating her!" Sweets said as she scooted between us, so she could be heard over the music. "He loves her! Trust me I know."

"Do you want me to snatch the back of your scalp to the front of your face?" he asked turning around to look at her. I turned the music down because it was obvious it wasn't working. Sweets ear hustling abilities were top notch.

"Well I suggest you sit back, be quiet and be cool. You don't want it with me. Trust me, honey! It won't be good!"

When she was in check he continued, "Then why would you allow him to tell you who to bring when you're hanging out with *your* girls? You're a grown ass woman."

"Cause I don't want to hear his mouth that's why. He's gonna be my future husband and I have to obey him."

"Obey?" he waved me off and said, "Stop at the store right there." He pointed his gold metallic finger nail at the 7 Eleven temporarily dropping the subject. "I have to pick up some ice but we will resume this conversation later."

"They have ice at the concert." I was growing increasingly irritated with him by the minute. "We really should stay on the

road."

"They ain't got enough for my world famous potato salad! Now go ahead it'll only take a minute."

I pulled up into the parking lot and told a pissed off Sweets we'd be right back.

I decided to go in with him because this man could shop, even if it was just 7 Eleven. And I didn't want him taking all day. I walked toward the ice chest and Miss Wayne went Gawd knows where. When I grabbed a bag I saw three dudes walk up to me.

"Dayum, ma! You sexy den a mofo!" one of them said as he licked his crusty bottom lip and gave his friend some dap. He must've thought he just said something inquisitive. They were eyeing me as if I was naked and I felt violated.

I knew I was sexy in my jeans by Deelishis designed for the girl with the tiny waste and fat ass. So what he was saying didn't move me at all.

"Yeah she cute as hell to be dark." One of them said.

I smiled because lately I'd heard that a lot. In fact, Smokes told me I was a sexy dark chick on a regular. Apparently Miss Wayne didn't like it because he popped up and said, "And what exactly does that mean?"

"What exactly does *what* mean?" He looked at Miss Wayne as if he'd lost his mind.

"What does it mean to be sexy to be dark?"

"It means she's a fine dark sister!" He eyed Miss Wayne as if he was a science project. All I could think of was Lord, please let us get outta here without any altercations. "And what you worried about it for fudge packer?"

Miss Wayne paid that comment no mind. He went right back to the comment he said about me being cute to be dark. I saw in his eyes that their comment pissed him off but I didn't know why. He was being nice. He was paying me a compliment. So why the hostility?

"Well dark or not she's hot so what you sayin' is dumb.

Hell you make it sound like most dark people are ugly but she was *The One* that got away. And since it's obvious your mamma never taught you any manners…allow me. That shit you just said was rude and wrong."

"This mothaphucka's straps bout to bust on his sandals and he gettin' in my business about some bullshit?" he laughed talking to his boys. "You can't be for real."

"Hold up!" I told him. "You disrespecting now!"

"It's okay, Miss Parade," he said interrupting me. "I'm tryin' to find out why he's lookin' at my feet? Let me find out you into men."

And what Miss Wayne did next made my mouth dropped. He cupped the dude's balls and squeezed them afterwards licking his lips.

That set him off. He attempted to punch Miss Wayne and I dropped the ice and reverted back to my Quincy Manor days. I knew I had a right like Tyson.

Whop!

He fell back against his boys and they tried to help him up. The ice bag ruptured on the floor and I saw drips of his blood fall on it like water paint. I waited for him to make a move, just one, so I could hit him again. But he remained in his friends arms like a new born baby. I guess he was seeing stars.

"Come on, baby." Miss Wayne grabbed my forearm. "Let's roll. We'll get the ice at the place."

"That's what I thought," I told him wishing we never came in to begin with.

When we got in the car it was silent for a minute. I don't understand why I always feel the need to fight. I know it's not ladylike and I try hard not to. But something in me clicks and sometimes it's better for me to handle things the best way I know how. By whippin' a bitch's ass! Maybe I should've enlisted in the army or something where my talents could be put to better use.

"What's wrong with you, Miss Parade?" He's the kind of

person who had to know *why* things were instead of leaving well enough alone. Besides, he knew full well why I dropped his ass on the floor.

"Because he was talkin' about you that's why."

"I'm not talkin' about what he said to me. My feet are big den a mothafucka in these shoes. I put a little too much salt on my pork chops last night and they swole up on me this morning. I wasn't bout to look for some different shoes to wear with this outfit so I decided to roll with them anyway. Nawl what I'm talkin' about is why would you accept him saying that you're cute to be dark?"

"Because he was paying me a compliment. You act like he said I was a ugly bitch or somethin'."

"He was."

"I didn't take it that way."

"Do you know what cute to be dark means?" Miss Wayne persisted.

"Naw explain it to me" I merged onto Route 29 leading to the concert.

"It means that normally dark women aren't cute and you were the *one* who made the exception. It's disrespectful and wrong, Parade. And it's far from a compliment!"

"I don't think it is." Sweets interjected. "If you look at TV nowadays, everyone is as light as me and you. Women, Parade's complexion aren't really cute at least the ones I've seen anyway."

"So are you actually sitting in the backseat of my friend's car saying she's unattractive?" he asked turning around waiting for her response.

"No! She's cute to be dark!" Sweets said seriously.

"You want the *Angelina Jolie's* don't you?" Miss Wayne asked as he peered at her.

"The *Angelina Jolie's*?" she repeated to be sure she heard him correctly.

"Yes…cause I'm about to swell your lips up three sizes too big if you don't sit back there and shut the fuck up."

Silence.

"Now, Parade that bitch in the back seat has lost her fuckin' mind but I haven't! There are plenty dark women who are gorgeous on TV."

"Name one." I asked.

"Name one?" he repeated looking confused and obviously trying to buy time.

"Just one. That looks like me that I can relate too."

I got him. There was not one single woman on TV that was considered attractive, with a complexion as dark as mine.

"But does that make you unattractive?" he finally replied not able to think of anyone.

"It seems like it." My words were too hard to swallow. "How can I feel good when everything I see on TV is contradictory to what I see in the mirror?"

"Parade…that's a question you're gonna have to answer. TV doesn't make who you are inside or out," he said softly touching my hand. "you do."

It was totally silent until, "Kimberly Elise!" Sweets blurted out covering her mouth quickly. She remembered Miss Wayne told her to be quiet but had forgotten.

"What?" we both said simultaneously.

She uncovered her mouth and said, "Kimberly Elise. She's on TV and you guys have the same complexion."

I knew who she was. She played Denzel's wife in John Q and she played in Tyler Perry's movie *Diary of a Mad Black Woman*. Still I didn't know if she was pretty enough for me. Or maybe because she didn't fit the description of what I was told pretty was.

"Yeah…I guess." I pulled up in Merriweather's parking lot.

"Kimberly Elise, huh?" Miss Wayne repeated shaking his

head looking at Sweets as we stepped out of the car. "Yous about a stupid, bitch!"

"I was just tryin' to help," Sweets said easing out of the car. "The truth is, Parade, you gonna have to stop lettin' everybody else's problem with your complexion be your burden. You are a woman. A beautiful one at that...and you have to start exuding that to everyone you meet."

Wow. Sweets got deep on me and for a second, she seemed different. Like she really cared. It was weird and made me somewhat uncomfortable because her words hit home.

"Girl, shut your fake ass up and come on!" Miss Wayne replied.

They were arguing and I needed to think. I allowed them to walk ahead of me to clear my mind. Cause I still wasn't convinced that the complexion I wore, wasn't the reason why everything went bad in my life, and it was going to take a miracle to change my mind. And God wasn't in the business of performing miracles in my life so I knew it would never happen.

Daffany

I'm watching TV and everything on reminds me of "*It*". I can't stop the urge and the desire I have to satisfy my ultimate craving. To get high. Not even the baby I carry in my womb makes the urge go away. At first the picture of Miss Wayne's bashed up face in my mind helps, but soon the violence he suffered because of me no longer works. Yet the only thing that holds me is that I know if I leave, Miss Wayne will come looking for me and I can't risk something happening to him…again.

I was able to get some dope from a white girl who lives in the next building over one day. I couldn't believe she let me get high with her. I guess misery loves company. I knew she was a dope head the moment I laid eyes on her. But after I told her I'd come back with my share of the money, and never did, she left me alone.

I decided to turn up the sound on the part in the movie *Stomp The Yard,* where Columbus Short danced off the song, "*Walk It Out*". That part always got me hyped and usually drew me into it. He looked like he owned the club when he moved on the stage. I remember when me, Parade, Sky and Miss Wayne use to hang out at the club. We use to own it too. I would always get high right before I went to put my mind at ease. But back then, I only fucked with Ecstasy.

High. High. High. High. High.

Yeah…*high*, that's what I want to be right now.

I jumped up and went to Miss Wayne's room looking for

some sweat pants and a baggy T-shirt large enough to cover my tummy. I needed to hide my pregnancy before I copped. Sometimes…not often…dealers didn't want to serve you if they had a conscious. I hated those types. My business was my business not theirs.

I didn't need this unborn baby stopping me from getting what I wanted, and sometimes I resented it. When I rummaged through his dresser, all I saw was tight pants, and girly clothes, none of which would fit over my stomach. And then I remembered, his lover Keith lived here too and always wore extra large clothes.

I made my way over to his side of the bedroom and accidentally hit my toe on the metal bed frame. Falling onto the bed I rubbed my toe until the pain subsided. This is crazy. What am I doing? It had been one day since I smoked and I want so badly to beat this thing. I just can't. Still, it feels good being able to walk around without it. For the first time in a long time I feel proud. I don't need that stuff. I can beat this! If I just try.

I got up on my way to return to the living room when I thought, *I could start over tomorrow*. Tomorrow I'll beat this thing for good and protect me and my baby. Yeah…my baby. *My baby*. What am I doing? I'm pregnant?!!!

"Lord please help me do this." I cried as I lay against the wall before sliding down into a ball on the floor. "I can't do this alone. I'm gonna kill my baby and I'm gonna kill myself too."

As I prayed for God to help me, I heard keys in the door. Did Miss Wayne forget something? I stood up and walked to the hallway and saw Keith walking in with two Louis Vuitton bags.

"Where's my, honey?" he asked locking the door after placing his bags down.

"He's at the concert." I told him as I took my place on the couch. I didn't want him coming in and controlling the TV like he usually did. He knew I didn't have a room and the only space I had was in the living room on the couch. Yet some days he

would bogart the TV and stretch out on the couch knowing full well I didn't have anywhere else to go in the apartment. And then when Miss Wayne wasn't home, he forbade me from going in his room. It's like he really didn't want me here or he wanted me to kiss his ass like it was his place. "Him and Parade left about forty minutes ago."

"He cook?" he eyeballed my full breasts.

"Yeah." I said focusing on the movie. He was making me uncomfortable. This was weird. Why is he staring at me like this? Prior to now I thought he didn't have any feelings for me either which way. So what changed?

"Won't you warm me up something to eat real quick?"

"Okay." I felt defeated as I handed him the remote. I guess me and my baby wouldn't have that plate in the microwave after all.

"I don't need the remote, I'm good." He sat it down beside him. "You can have the TV when you come back. Besides, I'd rather watch you instead."

Suddenly having the TV wasn't important to me anymore. I was lost and didn't know how to take him. I couldn't go into their room because I didn't belong. I couldn't stay out here because I would be in the way. I wish I never let my apartment go. I warmed up the plate and reluctantly placed it on the table in front of him.

"Salt?"

"Huh?" I responded wiping the water from rinsing his plate on my night pants.

"Where's the salt?" he asked digging into his meal finally taking his eyes off of me.

"Oh…I'm sorry, I'll bring it now."

I walked back in the kitchen trying to figure where I could go and who I could call. I was so far away from D.C. that nobody would want to pick me up. And outside of Miss Wayne, I didn't have any *true* friends. Everyone I'd associated myself with now was into drugs. I was trying to get away from everything but people make it hard. Keith is making it hard.

I placed the salt and pepper on the table and sat at the far end of the couch. With *Stomp The Yard* still on, I watched the part where the lead character in the movie introduced himself online after recently being accepted into the fraternity. I hoped and prayed Keith wouldn't do anything to compromise me and the love I had for Miss Wayne.

When he was done eating he said, "So how's the drug thing comin' along?"

"I'm doin' good." I explained looking at him briefly before returning my eyes to the moving objects on TV. I was no longer able to focus on what was going on or what was being said.

"Come sit by me," he said patting the cushion next to him.

"I'm good over here," I smiled looked at him briefly before turning away.

Reaching in my direction he repeated, "I said come sit next to me." He demanded grabbing my wrist.

I could tell he wasn't applying a lot of pressure now but my wrist still hurt. Didn't he know I was HIV positive? Or had Miss Wayne concealed it from him?

"I'm positive."

"What?"

"I'm HIV positive." I sat next to him like he requested. I was trembling. Next he forced me on my knees and I was directly in front of him.

"So am I." He smiled as he unzipped his pants stroking his extra large penis. "I just want you to suck it. And suck it good."

I knew he was lying about being positive and probably figured this was some sort of attempt to make him stop. It was, but I was also telling the truth. I'm HIV positive and if he per-

sisted, he'd be positive too.

"Please don't make me do this." I begged as he placed his hand behind my head, his penis completely out. "I love Miss Wayne and this would hurt him so much. He's my best friend."

"Okay," he smiled. "Just kiss it a little and I'll leave you alone. I just want you to wet my dick everyday with those pretty pink lips and we can consider your debt here paid. Okay?"

"What debt?" I cried trying to buy time.

"You don't think your living here isn't coming out my pocket too do you? I'm payin' your expenses too. It ain't just Wayne."

"But I can earn money. Please don't do this to me. Miss Wayne loves you!"

He grew hard in his hand before I even had a chance to do anything. The only thing he cared about was cumming. Keith was handsome. I couldn't understand why he was doing this to me. He could get any girl he wanted. Or any man for that matter.

"Shut the fuck up! You're talking too much!" He screamed and lines began to form in his forehead.

"I'm not doing it!" I pushed away from him and scooted backwards on the floor.

"Oh you want to be a disrespectful bitch!" He said leaping toward me. He was more than angry. He was furious!

Once he grabbed me, he spread my legs apart. On top of me, he pressed his body against mine and instantly my fighter instinct kicked in. I had to protect my baby! Not thinking, I put my fingers in his eyes and he screamed out in pain. After that I kicked him repeatedly with the soles of my feet while moving toward the door on my hands and knees. He jumped on my back weighing my stomach to the floor. He didn't care about me or my baby.

We rolled over and I ended on his stomach as he wrapped his arms and legs around me. Why was he doing this to me? This is crazy! Getting up off me, he tried to remove my pajama pants.

After a few thwart attempts to fight him off, eventually he's successful at pulling them down. With his dick in his hands, he moved for my pussy. I kicked him off again screaming my ass off. Somehow, by the grace of God I made it to the door. I ran as fast as I could and he couldn't catch me. I didn't look back. God! What now?!

Parade

The outdoor concert was crowded. People wore smiles as they sang along with the melodies of the artist. The sun shine on me warmly and I tried to place myself in the mood for life, love and happiness with my friend Miss Wayne.

I'm so happy we found a spot with enough room to spread out the quilt Miss Wayne brought, without everyone breathing on us. Suddenly I felt stupid for giving him such a hard time today for making sure we were prepared. This is what he always did. Cared for others. It was his gift. Because of him we could enjoy the concert as if we were looking at it from the comfort of our home.

"Uh…excuse me. But uh…can I share the quilt too? You knocking me over." Sweets asked as one ass cheek lay on the quilt and the other lay on the ground.

"Sure." Miss Wayne smiled. "You can sit on the one you brought with you." He pushed her further on the damp grass with his hips. "Now move!"

She pouted and sat on the grass crossing her legs. I shook my head because I never seen Miss Wayne throw as much shade as he did to her, with anybody else. He truly couldn't stand her and I wished he would tell me the real deal. Miss Wayne's not a hater and tends to bite his tongue to allow others to make their own mistakes. So what was different now?

"You've got this look I can't describe. You make me feel like I'm alive. When everything else is okay, without a doubt

you're on my side. Heaven has been away too long, Can't find the words to write this song of your love. Ohhhhhh your love....." Miss Wayne sang along with Corrine's melodic voice.

I put my head back and thought about my life and how things would be being married and filthy rich. A smile came across my face because my life is nothing like it use to be. Yet something was missing. And I was scared to find out what.

I felt on top of the world until I looked up and saw Jay. *Jay Hernandez*. My Jay! He was sitting in the row of seats right before me. His hairy arm was wrapped around the back of the girl's chair and she was kissing him softly on the lips. Her long black hair draped behind her seat like a beautiful curtain. Without looking at her face, I knew she was beautiful.

I felt a wave of sickness come over me. Suddenly any thoughts of happiness went out the window. How could he? He was mine! I don't care if I haven't been answering his phone calls or taking his visits. I cared about him. I needed him. I just didn't know it until now.

"Miss Wayne, I'll be right back." I stood up and dusted myself off.

"Okay but you're gonna miss the best part." He looked up at me and his beautiful eyes were worried.

"Yeah! This is your favorite song." Sweets reminded me.

"Girl, shut up!" Miss Wayne told her tapping her leg. "You're like a worrisome ass dog humpin' on my cankles (calf and ankles combined)." When he was done with her he looked up at me and said, "Hurry back."

I was already moving. Every step I took was difficult. It was like Jay was sitting on top of my head, physically. I was so shook I almost stepped on a few people sitting on the lawn enjoying the concert. Why can't I shake him? He is not good for me. Since the moment I laid eyes on him he belonged to someone else, my best friend at that. Still...I feel as if we were meant to be, almost as if we are soul mates. I want that man. I need that

man to hold me. To touch me. To kiss me.

"Can I have a bottled water please?" I told the cashier at the concession stand. I don't even know how I ended up here. I handed her a hundred dollar bill.

"You ain't got nothin' smaller?" She made me feel slightly embarrassed that I had a larger bill than she could break.

"No, because unfortunately…my man gives *everything* to me big." I said sarcastically waiting on her weak ass reply.

"Whatever!" She rummaged through the drawer.

"You know what," I said wanting to prove a point that money ain't nothin' but a thang to me. "Keep the change and by yourself some manners, bitch!"

I walked off and everybody looked at me in disbelief. It felt good because back in the day, my broke ass could ride off a C note for at *least* three weeks. My mind was on the cashier but my heart returned to Jay. I looked toward the chairs this time and didn't see him! All that appeared was her long flowing hair. Maybe he was under the seat eating her pussy, something he never did to me.

I was so busy thinking about him that I didn't see the group of girls in front of me.

"Excuse me." I was able to stop right before we collided.

"Black bitch!" I heard one of them say.

I stopped in my tracks, turned around and said, "What did you just say to me?!" as loud as I could to be heard over the music.

The three girls turned around. I felt like this was Dejavu. Except last time this happened, Sky, Miss Wayne and Daffany were by my side. Now I was alone.

"Come again." The brown skin tall girl said as she raised her brow and balled her fist.

"I said what did you just say to me?" I walked toward her. I needed someone to take my frustrations out on and she would be perfect. She was a fighter just like me and easily provoked. I

saw it in her eyes and I lusted after a good match!

"I don't know what you're talking about, sweetheart," she looked at me from my eyes to my toes. "but you should keep it moving."

"I'm not moving a motha fuckin' place!" I was now close enough to lay hands on this slut! "Why did you call me a black bitch?"

"Oh!" she laughed as her friends begin to giggle.

"What's funny, whore?" I felt as if I were being made a fool of.

"Whore?" She wiped the smile off her face. "First off your mother's not here and second off I'm laughing because we weren't even talking about you. I was talking about this girl over there I know."

I smiled and said, "For starters my mother *is* a whore," I told her needing to fight somebody. All of their mouths dropped due to hearing me talk about my mother and I wished I could take my comment back. "And I know you *were* talkin' about me and now I'ma make you eat your words."

I was just about to swing on her when I felt a chest behind my head and an arm around my waist. My hands dropped by my sides and my body felt weak. The smell of his cologne soothed me. It reminded me of a scene in the movie *Ghost*, where the dead took over bodies.

"You ladies have a nice day." The voice said as I fell back into his chest as if he sucked the negative energy from me.

They looked up at him and down at me. The main girl said, "You actin' like a fool when you pulled a nigga like that?" she laughed. "You betta calm down before somebody snatch pop his fine ass."

When they left I turned around and faced him. It was the first time I'd seen him up close since IHOP.

"What do you want?" I asked walking away.

"You." He grabbed my hand.

I stopped. I really didn't want to go. Nor did I want him to leave.

"How you want me when you came here wit' a bitch?!" I pointed in the direction she was sitting in waiting for him to say something I wanted to hear. Do you know how much I love this man? "So take your high yella ass on over there with your little whore."

"I saw you when you came in." He was unmoved by my attitude.

"You ain't see shit." I said folding my arms.

"First off you're with Wayne's ass whose about 6'2, light skin and wearing high heels. Ray Charles could spot yalls asses."

"So? You don't act like you knew I was here. Kissing on her and shit."

"I didn't know you were coming but I did know you were here. But what you want me to do? You won't take my calls." His voice was serious. "Then you change your number and every time I tell Wayne or Daffany to give me your new one, they ignore me. I figured you didn't want me around, Parade. Shit! How do you want me to act?"

"Don't get all sensitive on me now." I pretended as if I didn't want to hear one word he had to say. I had to break him down because everything he said just now made me emotional. If he told me he wanted me as much as I wanted him anymore I'd lose it. "Plus if you really cared you would've treated me right a long time ago."

"Parade," he said holding my hand before pulling me closer to him. "When you gonna stop playin' these games with me shawty? You feelin' me. I know it."

"Oh so you ain't feelin' me?"

"Yes. Why you think I'm over here when that girl could pull up on me at any moment? I'm a different dude, Parade I swear. Give me a chance before you judge me. Would the same dude you use to know be outside at a gay ass concert begging you?"

"Don't throw that girl up in my face cause you ain't nothin' but a cheatin' ass, nigga and that's what cheatin' ass niggas do. Leave their bitches alone."

"So what that make you?" He released me and I missed his touch already. "You cheated with me on Sky too. So stop throwin' that weak shit in my face. That ain't for us no more."

Silence.

"Now are you gonna continue to poke holes in my character or are you gonna give me a chance and stop runnin'?"

"I don't know, Jay! The timing is all fucked up." I turned around and focused on the big crowd behind us.

"Give me a chance, Parade. Come by my place tomorrow night and let's talk about it then. Aight?"

I nodded but wasn't sure if I *meant* yes or no. He kissed my lips softly and I could taste a hint of the mint gum he had in his mouth. Suddenly I wanted us to leave together. I can't believe I'm in love, with someone other than my fiancé. I heard that absence makes the heart grow fonder. I guess it's true.

It was a long ride back to Bowie and I wasn't anywhere near being able to rest. First I had to drop Miss Wayne off and then I had to take the hike all the way back home to Virginia. The only thing that kept me up was having Jay on my mind. Was I really going to meet with him tomorrow? And if so, what would that mean for us?

When we finally reached Miss Wayne's place I rested a little easier because I knew I was one step closer to getting in my bed.

"You want me to help you with these bags?" I asked a tired and sleepy Miss Wayne when we stopped.

"What you think?" He stepped onto his parking lot…shoeless. He'd taken his sandals off the moment we stepped

foot onto the concert grounds and hadn't put them back on since.

I put the car in park, got out and grabbed one of the bags. Sweets was sleep with her mouth wide open and she was sleep. Her ass was also laying on the other two bags.

"Sweets, get up." I told her as she leaned toward the other side of the car freeing the straps.

We walked all the way up his steps and he fumbled with getting his key out of his purse to open the door. He yawned and I yawned next. Instead of opening the door himself, it swung open and we saw Keith walking back to the couch with not so much as a hello. The living room was dark and all the lights were out with the exception of the one in the kitchen. *Damn they rude then a mothafucka in this apartment.* I thought.

"What's up, baby?" Miss Wayne said walking in looking around the apartment. I could tell he was looking for his precious little Daffany. He placed the picnic bag down first, his shoes next. "What you doin' home? I thought you weren't coming back until tomorrow." He continued looking in the back.

"What…you don't want me home?" he asked ruder than I ever heard him speak to Miss Wayne before.

"I'm sorry, honey." Miss Wayne acted as if it were all his fault. He kissed him gently on the cheek. "We had a long day and I'm tired that's all. Want me to make you something to eat?"

"I already ate."

"Aight Miss Wayne," I said placing the bags down. Keith was acting like a cunt and I hated hearing him talk to my friend that way. So I had to roll. "Give me a hug so I can get outta here." I mugged Keith slightly so he could see my displeasure but not too much for Miss Wayne to detect.

Miss Wayne hugged me back and released me.

I was twisting the doorknob and had one foot outside of the apartment when I heard Miss Wayne ask, "Where's Daffany?"

"I put her out." He said it like Miss Wayne asked him,

what time is it?

I stepped back inside, closed the open door and turned around. I wasn't sure if I heard him correctly. What did he mean he put her out? As far as I knew it wasn't his place to do so.

"What?! Why?!" Miss Wayne looked as if he were about to go into convulsions or something.

"She came on to me and I put her out." He replied calmly. "I wasn't feelin' comfortable with her staying here after that."

"See!" I said to Miss Wayne shaking my head. I circled around the small space in front of the door. I knew she would do somethin' like this being addicted to drugs! "I told you that bitch was not to be fucked with, Miss Wayne! You should've just listened to me!"

"Parade is right." Keith said agreeing with me. "Cause she sure did tell me she'd been wantin' me for a long time."

Miss Wayne sat on the couch with his face in his hands but I resonated on Keith's last statement. *Cause she sure did tell me she been wantin' me for a long time*. Daffany was many things, a whore and a drug addict included, but she didn't *lust* after anybody that didn't belong to her. She only did what she had to for money but would've never made such a comment. *Wantin' him for a long time?* Yeah right! Something wasn't right about this shit.

"So let me get this straight," I said slowly. "She said she's been wantin' you for a long time? Did she ask for any money?" I raised my brow in confusion and I wanted some answers.

"Nope. She only wanted sex."

By this time Miss Wayne was in tears until I said, "Yous a lyin', mothafucka!" There was no way she'd fuck any of these niggas for free. Not after what happened to her at a party we were all at when Sky was alive. This dude she was feelin' came on to her. But when he found out she slept around for money, he played her like a whore. And she was really hurt by it. After that she was one heartbreak away from being lesbian. And the only thing she

cared about now was getting high. Nothing else mattered to Daffany but dope, especially gay ass Keith!

"What?" Keith repeated as if he didn't hear me correctly. Guilt was written all over his face.

"I said yous a lyin', mothafucka! Daffany would never lust after yo ass when she knows how much this man loves you! If she did come on to you, it woulda been for money but not straight off some I want some dick type shit!"

Miss Wayne looked at me and then at him. I could tell in his face he got where I was going with it too.

"Exactly what happened?" Miss Wayne said his mood going from hurt to anger. He fixed his eyes on Keith and waited for his response.

Keith looked at me and fiddled around with the remote. When I looked at the TV I noticed it wasn't even on. Yeah! He's as guilty as sin! He was shook and couldn't conceal his nervousness. He was a rookie at this shit.

"I came home early lookin' for you," he started slowly looking at the floor and back at Miss Wayne. "And I noticed she was home. The first thing she said to me was *do you want something to eat*? In a seductive tone." I could tell he was thinking of his story as he went along. "I was like naw I'm good. And then she said something about eating something else instead."

Eating something else instead? Is he serious? Daffany don't even like her pussy ate! And what was she going to eat from him? His ass? This was some bullshit and I knew it! Me and Miss Wayne use to clown her on how bad she hated oral sex back in the day. And with her having HIV, she'da never put Miss Wayne into harms way like that. Drug cravings and all, I knew she'd reach down deep somewhere to prevent from putting him in that kind of jeopardy.

"You lyin'!" I felt like breaking his jaw. "Daffany don't even get down like that! And yous a, bitch ass nigga for sayin' that shit too!"

"I'm tellin' the truth!" he pleaded with me. "I told her I wasn't feeling what she was givin' and she got upset."

"Yo I'm 'bout to go upside this bamma head, Miss Wayne! This dude is trippin'! That don't even sound like Daffany!"

It was pissing me off because he was a cop and here he was straight lying on Daffany. He wasn't even that cute. Keith was skinny, extra red and had a goofy laugh. Daffany went for the smooth *Usher* types. Don't get me wrong, she's not herself right now, but she's not the person he's describing either.

"I want you out of here!" Miss Wayne yelled pointing his finger in Keith's frightened face. I could tell by the look in his eyes that he was aware of what Miss Wayne was capable of when provoked. Dude turned from police officer to scared little bitch in fifteen seconds flat.

"Baby…please…this is not my fault!" His hands were out in front of him trying to avoid any future slaps. "She's the one to blame not me."

"How long has she been gone?!" I yelled in the midst of him begging for forgiveness. This was making me sick and I was trying to find Daffany. I ain't have time for his lyin' bullshit!

"About thirty minutes ago. I can help you look for her if you want." He advised hoping that would win him some points. "It ain't even been that long since she left."

"Your, bitch ass, did enough!," I yelled pointing at him. "I'll be back Miss Wayne." I was preparing to leave. "But if I was you, I'd put this punk ass, nigga out your crib. But that's just me."

I jotted down the stairs as quickly as possible. Once I got in my car I sped off and looked up and down the street for Daffany. Sweets woke up asking me something but I couldn't hear her. I was seeing red and I was liable to kirk out on some-body right now. I hate how people use people weaker than them and I'd be damned if I was gonna let Keith get away with this

shit! He probably tried to rape her or something and she fought back.

I was starting to worry when I couldn't find her. This was a quiet neighborhood so somebody walking up and down the streets would be out of place. Sweets must've figured I was looking for somebody and said, "Is that who you're lookin' for?"

Daffany was barefoot and walking slowly with her arms folded in front of her. For the first time since I left Miss Wayne's I could breathe. I pulled up on her slowly and said, "Get in."

She stopped, looked at me and than hopped in the front seat. Daffany looked back at Sweets and then at me. She remained silent. No words passed between us until I pulled off.

"He gone yet?" She finally asked looking at the road ahead of us.

"He's on his way out now."

"You know he tried to rape me right?"

"Yeah. I figured as much."

"It's not my fault, Parade. I wasn't tryin' to do what he wanted me to." She said convincingly.

"I know. Why you think I'm out here lookin' for you? But I still think you're to blame for a lot of what's happening to you. You fell off, Daffany and hard too. I don't think I could ever forgive you for what you're doing to us right now. Still…," I continued pulling into Miss Wayne's parking complex. "You're not a sheisty person and don't deserve this."

"Thanks." She said looking at me before getting out the car. "P…Parade?" she said as if my name were a question.

"What's up?"

"I'm sorry about our fight. I didn't mean half of the shit I said to you. Sky getting killed hurts me. Everyday. I can't stop thinking about her. We argued before she was killed and I didn't get a chance to tell her how much I loved her."

"She knows," I said feeling the same way as Daffany. "We argued the last time I saw her too. But let's not talk about that right now." I remembered Sweets was in the car and I didn't want to talk about Sky being murdered, especially since she knew Smokes..

"But I am tryin' to change. I really am. I just need your help. Will you help me? *Please*?"

Silence.

"I don't know right now, Daffany. I got a lot to deal with in my own life. Maybe we'll talk later about your situation."

With that she took one last at me, got out the car and walked into the building.

Five minutes later while driving down the beltway thinking about everything that had happened, Miss Wayne called.

"Did you get her?"

"What you talkin' about?" I asked sleepily, the sounds of Sweets snores in my ear.

"I said did you find Miss Daffany?

His statement although simple terrified me. Why was he asking me if I found Daffany when I'd dropped her off a while ago? When I glanced down, I saw Daffany's keys on my car seat. She never had no intentions on going back. As much as I hated lying to him, I couldn't hurt him anymore with the truth either. Daffany was a lost cause. And I couldn't participate in this massacre of his heart any longer.

"No. I never found her."

I stayed on the phone and listened to him cry, until I pulled up in my driveway.

Jay

PRESENT DAY

Jay and Zeeway were in Georgetown in D.C., getting some custom made jewelry at his regular spot. The place was jumping with dealers and people who just had an obsession for jewelry. Although Jay was with Zeeway, his mind was on Parade and he couldn't wait to see her later on that night. And he hoped she wouldn't call him with any bullshit.

"Listen…I want fifteen diamonds around the bezel of this Gucci watch. And don't fuck it up!" Zeeway yelled to the Asian attendant. "I know how ya'll mothafuckas be some time."

"I hear you the first time," the Asian woman said.

"Easy, man," Jay interrupted. "You gonna fuck up my relationship with these peoples. They gonna look out. I always come here. Chill out."

"Yeah whatever," Zeeway said waving him off and dismissing the attendant after reluctantly handing over his watch. "So what's up with that bitch? You hit yet?"

"What bitch?"

"The broad I saw you with last night. You hittin' that or what?"

"Nigga, don't worry about it," Jay laughed brushing his

dumb ass off. "I got this."

"I bet."

"But what's up wit you and Smokes? You get wit him about your money yet?"

"Yeah…but this nigga on some other shit B," Zeeway said scratching his head. "Yo doing some other shit I ain't with. Peep this," he said looking around. "I think he about to put his bitch on to the game. At one point I thought he was wifin' her but now I see that nigga grimier than me!" he laughed. "but fuck these hoes out here! Put em all to work for all I give a fuck!"

Jay was heated. His feelings for Parade had grown solid ever since she cut him off for treating her like shit back in the day and he didn't want to see anything bad happen to her. Or good for that matter if he wasn't involved.

"What you mean?" Jay asked his nostrils flaring.

Zeeway saw his expression and figured he said too much. Smokes had told him time after time to watch his tongue, yet it constantly hung out of his face.

"Nothin', nigga," he responded trying to get out of his blunder. "Enough talkin' bout bullshit. I'm trying to get somethin' to eat."

Right before the conversation continued, a beautiful specimen with long black hair walked into the shop. Her beauty was stunning and Zeeway immediately took notice. She favored Megan Goode greatly.

"Yo look at shawty," Zeeway said looking tapping Jay's arm while looking at her. "I'm bout to go holla."

"Hold fast on that shit," Jay stopped him. "What did you mean about Smokes putting his bitch on?"

"Nothin', nigga," Zeeway barked. "Relax!" he had a feeling he was fucking Smoke's chick for sure and wondered if that was the female he saw in the car the other day. "I was just talkin' shit."

Jay was enraged. He couldn't even pretend like he was-

n't. He decided to bounce on his dumb ass. But before leaving he made an observation about the female he was sweating.

"Aight, yo! I'm out," he smiled devilishly while Zeeway was rapping to the girl. "But just so you know," he said looking at the chick. "That bitch you talkin' to is a dude!"

The smile was wiped clean from Zeeway's face. And just like that, Jay was out.

Parade

CURRENT DAY

I was inside of the shower nervously wondering if Zeeway would come over today and blast my shit wide open. Would he recognize me even if he didn't see my face? He finally made contact with Smokes and I was scared to meet him in person. Then I wondered if I could get away with seeing Jay again today unnoticed. Why did I agree to meet him at his house? Hell…I already knew the answer. I was addicted. I was thirsty. And only Jay could quench my thirst.

"Parade! Parade!" I heard Smokes yell while the water flooded my ears. I turned off the faucet and wiped my soapy eyes to be sure he was calling me. "Parade! You hear me?!"

"Yeah, baby! What's up?" I said with my hands resting on the faucets ready to turn the water back on once I found out what he wanted.

"When you get out of the shower get dressed and come to the living room, I got somebody I want you to meet."

Oh shit! I know its Zeeway. This is crazy! He's gonna see my car from last night and then remember. What was I thinking? Why was I taking such a risk on a man who never loved me to begin with? Jay was already proving to be more trouble than he was worth. I was about to lose my mind until I remembered I

parked the car in the garage, instead of the curb like I usually did. So unless they went in there, it would be impossible for him to see it. Thank God! Now all I was gonna have to do is get out of the house.

"Okay, baby." I turned on the water to cause a diversion in case I started talking to myself out loud.

I got out of the shower and the soap suds from my shower clung to my body. I dried myself off and eased on my panties. Wiping the steam from the mirror with my hands I was able to look at myself.

Pushing irrelevant thoughts out of my mind, I thought about Zeeway again. I wasn't sure but something told me things were getting ready to get out of hand. I'm getting ready to lose everything. I just know it.

Smokes

Can I talk to you please?" Sweets asked as she entered Smoke's house.

"I got company." He advised opening the door. His muscular chest was visible despite the white wifebeater t-shirt he was wearing.

"Please," she insisted. "It'll only take a moment."

He wiped his bald head with his hands and slid in the living room with his O.Dawg slippers on his size 13 feet. Letting out a heavy sigh he said, "Make it quick."

Sweets 's eyes met Zeeway's as she followed behind Smokes. He stopped in the living room within listening distance from his company.

"Can I talk to you in private?" she added looking at Zeeway who was looking her up and down. The hairs on the back of her neck stood up when he rubbed his dick and licked his lips as he eyed her in the doorway.

"Aight…let me talk to him right quick. You go wait in the den."

She did as she was told and Smokes walked over to Zeeway.

"I see you got a lot of shit goin' on around here. You sure you can handle both of them? Or do you need my help?"

"I know you betta keep your voice down before that bitch comes out and hears you."

"My bad."

"Now what did you have to tell me?"

"Oh…yeah," Zeeway said remembering their earlier conversation. "I think Jay's fuckin' her for real. I saw your car over his crib last night and at first I wasn't sure, but when I saw it when we were in the garage, I was certain."

Smokes looked irritated but knew all a long she was with him. He was angry because he couldn't control her, not because she was stepping out on him. He had to make sure she was niave enough to get on the plane that had her name all on it. And if Jay stayed around, it would be difficult for her to do.

"Let me worry about that," Smokes said. "You just play him close and keep your ears open. Now let me check her real quick," he continued referring to Sweets.

He bounced toward the den.

"What's so important it can't wait?" Smokes asked. "Parade is here so this can't be too long."

"I don't think you need Parade as much as you think you do." She said sitting on the grey plush sofa.

"How many times I gotta tell you," he said closing the door and than sitting beside her. "We need her. Be patient! Why you trippin?"

"Smokes this shit is pissin' me off. If you want to be with me let me help you. Trust me to do whatever it is you say she has to do. Why we got to play games with this bitch while you play me off as her maid? I can handle whatever you need her to do if you would just talk to me."

Smokes looked angrily upon her until his facial expression changed. Instead of yelling he planted a passionate kiss on her lips. He knew what she needed. Women always tripped when they didn't get a good dose of dick and she was no exception. Their tongues danced until he took control and sucked hers softly. She dropped her purse on the floor and fell back onto the couch. His body covered hers as he removed his dick and pulled her skirt up. Her panties cutting against her soft pussy lips hurt at first, until he fucked her like she wanted to be fucked. Her mouth opened and she almost moaned aloud until he covered her lips with his hand.

Smokes had one thing on his mind. Control. And if he had to fuck this bitch on a regular to get her to chill and stop tripping, he was willing to do what he had to do. Besides, he really did like her and he knew she'd do whatever he needed done when the time was right.

"Shit! Your pussy good as shit!" he let out as he pulled his dick out and released his semen on her sweaty body. Just when he did, Parade opened the door.

"Get the fuck out!" he yelled right before she opened it all the way, exposing their indecencies.

Parade slammed it shut missing their sex scene by seconds. They both hurried up and got themselves together. He didn't care if Sweets reached a climax or not, he was almost caught and it was all her fault.

"Now listen. We got to do what we go to do until everything is done. When I'm ready to let you in on everything you'll know. Until then, you gotta trust me and keep an eye on this bitch for me," he said breathing heavily. "Can I count on you or what?"

"Yes." she said adjusting her clothes, his sperm and her cum stuck to her skirt. She looked at the door once more to make sure Parade wasn't coming back in. "You can count on me."

"Good…that's what I want to hear."

Parade

What the fuck was that about? When I walked into the living room, Zeeway told me Smokes was in the den, and when I went to see him, he screamed at me before I could walk in. Something was up and I was uneasy.

Walking back in the living room, I caught Zeeway's stares. Wearing a pair of tight fitting blue jeans and a short Juicy top that showcased my fit abs, I put a little extra in my step so he'd continue to look at my body and not my face. He did everything I wanted him to do. His mouth dropped as he saw the flatness of my stomach and the fatness of my ass.

And seconds later, Smokes walked out. I walked over to Smokes and planted a passionate kiss on him and then I wrapped my arms around his neck. When I did, I saw Sweets standing behind him.

"Is everything okay?" I asked my eyes fixated on Sweets.

"Yeah…Sweets was just leaving," he said nonchalantly. Without saying a word, she walked out the door. When she was gone, Smokes directed his attention toward me. But I wanted to know what happened in the den. Part of me cared but the part that loved Jay could give a fuck! I just wish if he did want to be with her, that he'd let me go.

"Zee, this my future wife." He said changing the subject. "Parade."

I extended my hand and he accepted, holding it longer than he should have. My plan had exceeded my expectations. He

was so consumed with lust that he didn't even realize that we'd been in each other's presence before. Done with my game, I decided to excuse myself.

"Baby, I'ma step out real quick." I told him as I kissed him one last time on the cheek.

"Where you goin'?" he asked holding me tighter around my waist.

"Just hangin' with Miss Wayne and them," I lied.

"Bet…bet…," he said releasing me and then rubbing his head. He then looked at Zeeway who smirked. What the fuck was that supposed to mean? "Call me when you get there. I want to talk to you about something."

"You got it, daddy."

Not wanting to be around Zeeway too long, I ran out of there so fast I almost fell on the cement. I had to get to Jay. All day I've been thinking of him. The way he talks to me…and the way he holds me…all move me.

"I'm on my way." I told Jay on his cell phone as I jumped in my ride and backed quickly out the driveway.

"Good…I got a surprise for you." Jay responded sexily.

"And what surprise is that?" I wanted to keep him on the phone a little longer just to listen to his voice.

"Well if I tell you I'll have to kill you."

"You'd kill me?" I asked him playfully. "How we gonna have fun if you do that?"

"Naw…but I'd murder that pussy!"

"I'll be there in five minutes." I hung up before my pussy got unnecessarily wet before I saw him.

Everything about this is wrong. But I hung up with him and hit the gas. I made a decision that today…I'm not engaged and I don't belong to anybody but Jay, the original love of my life. Yeah he's fucked up. I already know he is. But…still…there's something about him that I simply must have. At any cost.

I blasted my Neyo CD and let number 11, "*Say It*" play over and over in my ear. About thirty minutes later I was sitting outside of Jay's place waiting, parked next to his car. With my right knee vibrating I pressed my hand on it to stop it. Unbuckling my seatbelt, I quickly moved toward his building and knocked on the door. No answer. I knocked again. Still no answer. His car was there so he had to be home. I glanced down at my watch and got irritated. He was late. Why wasn't he here when I just spoke to him? I called him several times and he didn't answer his phone. It took fifteen minutes of no Jay for me to realize he played me. I was in my car with the seat belt buckled preparing to leave when I heard a loud roar. Looking out my rearview mirror, I saw someone pulling up with a lime green Ninja motorcycle. I knew enough to know it was a 900 cc or larger.

The large motorcycle pulled up right next to me and its loud roar made me uncomfortable. I wondered who he was until he removed his helmet and I saw Jay's beautiful face. A black and white scarf dressed his head. He took it off and placed it in the back of his jeans.

"You ready?" he asked looking into my car.

"You can't be serious?" I got out. His mouth dropped when he got a look at the curves of my body.

"Uh…yeah…I'm serious." He handed the spare helmet. "We ridin' out on this tonight."

"I'm not messin' with you on no bike, Jay." He stood up and placed the bike on the kickstand.

"Let me find out you scared." He laughed holding his helmet under his arm. "Not Miss-I– beat -a-bitch-down."

Without even talking I got on the front of the bike and said, "Get on."

"You real cute. Stop playin' girl," he laughed. "You don't know shit 'bout ridin' no motorcycle. Just slide that phat ass behind me and enjoy the ride."

He was still running his mouth when I hopped on, removed the kickstand and revved the engine. He didn't know as much about me as he thought he did. Living in Quincy Manor hanging around guys and being a tomboy had its perks. I knew how to ride everything from dirt bikes to motorcycles.

Jay eased behind me hesitantly and wrapped his arms around my waist. And to make him feel comfortable about a woman taking the lead, I backed my ass into him. Immediately he got hard. I don't care who Jay's been with…nobody fucked him the way I did. I was certain.

"You know this shit is sexy right?" he said loudly over the bike's engine.

"If you like that I got somethin' else to show you later." I kicked the gear from neutral, to first and beyond.

And just like that we were gone. I knew he was impressed with the way I maneuvered on the roads and Baltimore Washington Parkway. I seemed fluid. Just seeing the beautiful trees and feeling the air against my body with someone I obviously still loved had me aroused. Love? I swallowed hard at the realization of my thoughts. If my heart belonged to him, what was to become of me and Smokes?

Damn!

Daffany

Where am I? I lie on the floor of an apartment with nothing but a mattress in the corner. How did I get here? As I try to stand, I noticed I felt a little off balance so I lean up against the wall for support. Nothing about this place seemed familiar. I was just about to twist the doorknob when I heard voices. Placing my ear against the wooden door, I listened as best I could.

"How much you gonna pay me for her?" one voice asked.

"I don't know. She's kinda busted and I might not be able to get a lot for her now. So if you really want to get paid, you might as well let me take her off your hands."

"Take her off my hands? She's pregnant! You know niggas pay extra for that kinda pussy. Give me a thousand or I'm taking her back."

They're talking about me? My heart beat rapidly in my chest as I wondered how I got here. My bare feet pressed against the wooden floor and the only thing I was wearing was a white t-shirt and some filthy pink panties. God please help me. Please help me.

"You've lost your fuckin' mind! I'm not payin' you more than six hundred for that doped out bitch! You lucky I'ma give you that!"

There was silence. Was my life being auctioned out there? Were they actually talking about me? Tears ran down my face and I wiped them off with my hand. And when I rubbed them together, they felt gritty. Like they needed to be washed.

"Aight…give me seven hundred and you can keep her."

"I told you my price. Six hundred or get her funky ass outta here."

"Fuck it! I'll fuck her myself before I let you get me like that," he said angrily. "All that fuckin' trouble I went through to get her back! I even had to bust that faggy ass nigga in the head for her a while back. She finally came back and I be damn if I'm lettin' her go for that amount."

I knew exactly who he was now. I'd deal with him from time to time to get some money to feed my habit. He was always mean but he always paid. Most of the time he paid me with dope.

I heard his feet scurrying in my direction and I lay down on the mattress. I was scared. Nervous! Is this how the slaves felt when their lives were exchanged without their consent? I didn't even have enough strength to bolt out the doors and fight for my life. The door opened and a little bit of light snuck through.

Just before they entered the room, the other said, "Let's talk." And the door closed. What was to become of me now?

Miss Wayne

Tyson's Corner in Virginia, was busy as usual. Some window shopped while the rich ignored price tags on their pursuit of glamour. I was calm as I placed the three Louis Vuitton purses retailed at over $8,000 dollars on the counter. I had done this so many times it was natural.

"How are you going to pay for these, sir?" she asked looking at me like I was stealing. Which I was. "Cash, check or charge?"

"I'll be charging these." I slid the card Visa card towards her.

I had five orders to place and the purses were the last ones on the list. Once I got these, I'd be done for a few months. The woman placed the designer purses in the bags and swiped the credit card. I waited patiently thinking about what I was going to cook for dinner. The card being declined was never even an option. I only used a card the day I received it and never, *ever* beyond 24 hours. So this card was brand new and ready to be used repeatedly.

"Excuse me, sir," she smiled. "There appears to be something wrong with the card. Let me make a phone call."

"Try it again," I advised, not trying to get others involved.

"It'll only be a second, sir," she assured me. "We like to make sure there's no fraud when we get this particular code. Don't worry, it's probably because of the amount."

"I don't know what the problem could be," I slid over my fake ID, which she failed to ask for initially, as proof. "My limit is over $50,000."

"One moment please," she said flinging one finger in the air ignoring my suggestion.

The way I saw it I had two choices. Wait for her to tell me that everything was fine only to have the cops waiting outside or run like hell. Sweat formed on my forehead for the first time ever. I was becoming nervous and something told me this would be it for me. So while she talked on the phone with her back faced my direction, I jetted. And trust me, when I ran, nobody could catch me, baby. I pushed over a few people and mushed one man in the forehead in a struggle to exit.

And then I heard, "Sir! Sir!"

I turned around to see who was calling me. It was the sales clerk and she was holding the bag in the air while waving my credit card.

"You forgot your bag."

What? I forgot my bag? I looked at the few people I pushed to get away, trying to determine if this was a set up. And then I thought about it. With those bags I'd get at least four grand tonight. Plus she still had my card which was good for the rest of the day. Slowly I eased over to the counter apologizing to my victims along the way.

"You seemed as if you were in a hurry," she smiled handing me the bag and my identification. "Turns out there was a technical error with the system, but everything's okay now."

I snatched the bag and my cards and said, "No problem. I was just on my way to the restroom. But I can hold it."

Once I got my shit I left. I knew I was going to have to find a new profession. This credit card shit had my nerves on edge. Between this and Miss Daffany not coming back home despite Miss Parade going to look for her, I was becoming an old hag. The one thing I needed, I knew I wouldn't be able to get. A

stiff dick. Even that was gone with Keith outta the picture. Lawd please help me before I lose my mind.

Parade

I hadn't planned on going to Jay's mother's house. And the moment we got off the bike I wanted to get back on and leave him standing. I knew she didn't like me and most of all I knew why. She liked the skin color to remain light in her family. And even though she married a black man before he divorced her ass, he was so light he could pass for white himself.

"Jay, I don't know about this," I told him as we stood in front of her home. The large apple tree to my left, the neatly trimmed bushes and beautiful green landscape did nothing to ease my stress. "I thought you said your mother was particular about the women you brought home."

"I know…but I'm feelin' you, Parade. And I want her to meet you. Let me worry 'bout all that other shit."

"But we not together, Jay. I mean…what's the point of meeting her? All we are-are sex partners who haven't even had sex in a while," I paused looking into his eyes. "Right?"

"Parade, don't fuckin' play wit' me. You and I both know what's up and pretty soon you goin' realize it too. Why else would we be here? I don't bring anybody to my mom's unless I know. Only one other person met her and that's it."

"And who was that? Sky?" I pouted.

"Let's not talk about it."

"Jay, this is confusing. You got me messed up right now," I said rubbing my forehead. "I don't understand. You worked so hard at making me feel like falling for you would be somethin'

you wouldn't want and now we're here."

"We're thinking too much right now, baby." He pulled my hand and led me toward the front door. "Let's just go with the flow. For right now, I want to go in here and have some of my mother's Spanish rice. Aight?"

"Aight," I smiled hesitantly.

He knocked on the door twice before it flew open. A beautiful Spanish woman with long shiny black hair opened the door and embraced Jay lovingly.

"Venido aqui cada uno! Jay aqui!" she said as she squeezed him.

"Hola mami!" he told her hugging her back.

I knew instantly that his family loved him when a few others ran out the door to embrace him. There was his mother, an elderly woman and a beautiful girl about sixteen. They were all Spanish and I couldn't help but feel overwhelmed by their beauty and light skin. I was there for a minute before he acknowledged me. But it was okay because I was use to being invisible.

"Ma…I have someone I want you to meet," he said breaking away from her affection. His mother was smiling until she laid eyes on me. "This is Parade Knight. And she's a special friend of mine. Real special." She stared at me as I extended my hand. Then she looked back at Jay. I didn't know what to do.

"Ma…shake her hand," Jay demanded feeling my uneasiness.

"Oh…uh…I'm sorry, baby," she finally accepted my hand. "I was so happy to see you that I lost my manners. "Welcome, Parade. Please come in." she said giving me a fake smile and an even faker introduction as she opened the door for me.

When I walked in, I saw her wipe her hand on her pants after she touched me. That hurt. I wouldn't say anything now, but I'd probably say something to Jay about it later. I just wanted to leave. Just go home. I hated being here.

When I walked in, there was so much furniture it was difficult to move. Most of it was wooden and she had a whole lot of porcelain statues all over the place. The biggest was in the shape of Jesus on top of the entertainment center. There were also rosaries on the corner of almost every picture including the one of Jay when he was younger. I smiled when I saw his picture. He had to be in middle school and I wondered how he would've treated me back then. The smile wiped from my face when I felt I already had my answer. He would've hated me. Just fingered me in dark corners and threw rocks at me in public. And I would've let him.

We stepped into the kitchen dining room and the elderly lady and the kids kept staring at me. I tried to focus on the meal to appear busy but the longer I stayed, the more uncomfortable I became. Eventually we found ourselves at the table and in front of a huge spread of food. The meal consisted of Spanish rice and chicken with rolls. She also had a large salad on the table with Italian dressing next to it. We were there for twenty minutes and still I didn't feel comfortable. They all laughed and joked and I could tell Jay was trying to include me in their conversations but it was obvious that the mother didn't like me. And I didn't like her either.

"So, Parade, how do you know Jay?" she finally asked me with a mouth full of rice. She fiddled with the rest of the food on her plate with her fork.

"I told you, ma," Jay interjected. "She lives in my complex."

"I see," she said eyeing my skin. "So she's *just* a friend."

Jay looked at me and I waited for his answer.

"She's more than just a friend, ma." I was surprised and it made me feel even closer to him.

"How so? She's a little darker than your taste isn't she?"

I don't remember what happened after she made her statement. I don't know how the Spanish rice ended up in her

face, and the chicken on the floor. All I knew was that I had his mother's face between my thighs as I wailed on her head. People were trying to pull me off and I couldn't tell who was who. Nor did I care.

I was just tired, angry and mad at people for judging me because of my complexion. All my life I've been persecuted or treated badly because of my skin. And I was starting to hate people…I was starting to hate everyone…and I decided to take it out on his mother.

"Get this black bitch outta my house, Jay! Now!" she screamed as she fought wildly with her back flat on the floor.

"I don't want to be here anyway!" I told her.

When she said that I was brought back into reality as Jay lifted me off of his battered mother. My feet didn't touch the floor as he hoisted me up. The front door appeared to be moving toward me at a rapid speed. I didn't touch ground until I was outside.

I stood there waiting to fight him too, if he wanted it. I knew I was out of line and a part of me wanted to apologize but I didn't feel like now was the time to admit my wrongs. Instead, I remained still with my arms folded in front of me. Jay looked like he wanted to kill me yet there was something holding him back. He made large pacing circles in front of me like he was trying to stop from knocking me out.

"Hold up," he started breathing heavily. He stopped in front of me and stared at the ground but not at my face. "Did you…," more heavy breaths, "just hit my mother?"

"Take me home, Jay!" I wasn't feeling the bullshit or the explanation. He should've never brought me here in the first place. "I just wanna go home that's it."

"Parade…why would you put your hands on my mother?" He finally looked at me. He looked hurt and confused.

"Jay, I don't have time for this shit!" I repeated pointing in his direction careful to keep my distance. "You shoulda neva brought me here knowing how your mother felt about me. Now are you gonna take me home or not?"

Jay didn't say anything right away. Just stared at me crazy like. His silence made me nervous and I decided there was no way I was getting on the back of that motorcycle with him.

"I'll walk! Fuck it!" I said before realizing I didn't have my purse. I hated that she was the reason Jay may have treated me so badly in the past. Maybe if she wasn't so racist, me and Jay could've been. "Jay...can you get my purse?" Before he could answer his mother opened up the door and threw my purse in my face, yelling something in Spanish.

"Get your black ass off of my steps!" she continued in English.

I was about to snatch that bitch through the door and beat her ass again but she closed it before I could and Jay blocked my path.

"You know what, Parade," he said with his hand up still flushed. "Just...just."

He didn't finish his statement, just walked inside. Now here I was stuck out in the middle of Bowie looking foolish. I picked my purse off the ground and walked away. Why did I even play the fool? Why was I so stupid for a man who made it obvious that he never loved me?

Walking up to his motorcycle, I was about to kick it but decided against it. I didn't want any of them thinking I was tripping. So I walked away, to where, I didn't know. I just needed to go.

Miss Wayne

So I'm in a nail salon getting some work done on my feet, when I get Miss Parade's frantic phone call. What on earth is going on with my family? I feel like I'm losing control with no help in sight. And I'm somebody who always has control! But you know what? I can't feel sorry for myself right now. They need me.

"I'm on my way, Miss Parade. Just stay put." I hung up and reached for my purse which was sitting on the floor. Taking my foot out of the salon bowl, my entire size 13 foot brushed the small Chinese woman's face by accident. She was giving me a pedicure when Miss Parade called me to say she needed a ride. "Sorry, honey. But I'ma have to get up," I told her trying to get myself together. I couldn't believe Miss Parade just said she hit Jay's mother!

"You pay first!" the small woman said as I struggled to get both feet safely out of the large sauna type bowl, and on the floor.

"I ain't got no problem payin', missy." I finally got both feet flat on the ground. "But you ain't do all the work so you only get half the money." I placed my hand on my hip.

"You pay full amount or else!" she said shaking her finger in my face.

"Bitch, I said you'll get your money but not all of it. Now if you'll excuse me."

The small woman frowned and looked at me as if she

wanted to scratch my eyes out. And you know what she had the nerve to do? Put her hand on my arm as to restrain me. That was a mistake!

"Miss thang, if you don't remove that wretched paw you call a hand off my arm, I'ma beat your lil ass silly!"

"You do nothin'!" she said as she pushed me against the wall causing a picture of a white woman showcasing her red nails by holding an apple to fall to the floor. It wasn't long before I also slid down. The picture cracked and my ass flopped twice before finally stopping. A few people stared at me and I felt like an idiot.

Now this bitch is about to get the business. I got up off the floor quickly planning to kill her. I'm gonna kill this bitch. And just before I wrapped my hands around her tiny throat, Miss Parade called again. I grabbed the phone keeping my eyes fixed on this maniac.

"Did you leave yet? Or do I have to be Daffany just to get some attention from you?"

"I'm on my way, Miss Parade! Calm down!" I told her eyeing my incomplete pedicure. "Just stay put." When I was done I threw ten dollars in the woman's face. "You're one lucky, bitch! I almost kicked your ass up in here. You betta thank God for a woman name Parade!"

I quickly put my gold sandals on which looked bad for a girl with a bad toe job. Then I rushed out the door and jumped in my ride.

"Miss Parade, what happened?" I asked the moment she stepped foot inside of my silver Mercedes Benz G-Class truck. "And why are you at Jay's mother's house beating her ass?"

Miss Parade got in, slammed the door and buckled her seatbelt. At first I was angry for how she was acting but after looking at her face, I knew she was hurt. The last thing she need-

ed was me wailing on her about slamming my car door.

"Miss Parade? Do you wanna talk?" I asked softly, driving down the road. "I'm here for you. I know you know that."

"Are you?" she said angrily with her arms folded on her chest. "I come to realize that everybody who says they're really here for me is not. And it's starting to make my skin crawl. I'm sick of my life and letting people into it! I'm sick of all this shit!"

I gave Miss Girl a chance to vent but I was getting ready to slap her into yesterday's news. I have *always* been there for her! *Always*! But it seems that ever since Miss Sky was murdered, she turned into some sort of bitch to replace the bitch Miss Sky use to be. Maybe she felt like she had to be tough for us since we'd been use to it from Miss Sky for so long. Maybe she felt like being a bitch would make people hate her since she didn't feel like she deserved to be loved. Who knows.

"Miss Parade, I don't know what happened with you and Jay, but don't ever talk to me like that," I said calmly. "I have always been there for you, and honestly, I'm tired of telling you that. If you would just trust me, and know that my friendship is here to stay, and that I'm real and would never leave you, we could get past this shit. What will it take for you to believe me, honey? What will it take for you to understand that I love you and will never leave your side?"

She didn't say anything. But as we drove down Landover road in Maryland in silence, the street light radiated on her tears. I was just about to pull over and hug her when I saw a pregnant lady, with no shoes on pushing a shopping cart down the road in what appeared to be a blue hospital gown. Another girl followed her pulling an empty baby's stroller.

"What the fuck?!" I said out loud.

"What? What's going on?" Parade said wiping her tears looking in the direction I was focusing on.

I didn't answer, just whipped my car over on the side of the road. It was Miss Daffany. Once in park, I was preparing to leave out until Miss Parade said, "Let her be. She doesn't want help Miss Wayne. You have to let her go."

I fanned her away like a fly and hopped out of the car. I couldn't believe that was my baby walking down the street like a zombie. She was so thin now it was a wonder how she was able to walk without breaking her own bones. She looked fragile and dirty. Tears fell down my face.

"We gonna make some money off of them pampers," the bitch who was with her said. "My aunt alone will pay money to take all of these up off us."

"Well let's hurry up. I'm tryna get high!" Miss Daffany responded not realizing I was behind her.

"Miss Daffany, what's going on?" I asked as I stood on the sidewalk and eyed her. With my hands on my hips, I couldn't believe the sight. She was a hot ass mess.

But when Miss Daffany looked at me, she backed up as to protect the cart. I guess she didn't know who I was and thought I was trying to steal it from her. The drug had already proven to be hard on her because her skin was becoming dry and her lips were cracked. I couldn't help but focus on my God baby she was carrying in her belly. And quietly I prayed to God to help us out of this.

"Miss Daffany, it's me, Miss Wayne." I told her softly. When I thought it was okay, I walked up to her. Her face was beaten badly and she looked ill. "What are you doing out here with no shoes on? And what happened to your face?"

"Come on, Daffany!" the girl interrupted. "He just tryin' ta get our pampers to sell 'em for hisself."

"Bitch, shut your baldheaded ass up!" I pointed my recently manicured nail in her face. "Fo I snatch what's left of that scalp out of your head."

Silence.

"Miss Daffany, what are you doing out here, baby? And who hurt you? I've been looking for you everywhere!"

Finally recognizing me, she threw her hands around my body. And although she smelled and looked bad, I was happy there was a moment of recognition.

"I been lookin' for you too! I ran away from someone who was tryin' to sell and beat me. It was the same one who hit you that time when you and Dayshawn helped me from the house. Where have you been?" Her eyes were glossed over and she looked half dead.

I sighed.

"I been at home, Miss Daffany. And I want you to come home with me now."

"I wanna come home, Miss Wayne." She looked at her bare feet. I took pity on her. It was as if she'd become a child right before my eyes. Where did the strong Miss Daffany I knew when I was younger go? "I'm scared! And I ain't got nobody to help me."

"What you talkin' bout? I help you all the time!" the bitch interrupted.

That's it! I'm sick of her shit! I took my left hand and smacked the hell out of her. Her knees buckled but somehow she prevented herself from falling to the ground.

"Say one more mothafuckin' thing and they'll be another one where that came from." I warned her.

Theoretically I don't beats women but this bitch was standing in the way of me saving my family. I believed strongly that if she wasn't in the picture, none of this would happen because Miss Daffany would've saw what it was like to be alone. And because she *was* in the picture, I would have to undue all of her dirty work.

"If you come home with me," I said softly holding Miss Daffany's gritty hand. "I'll take care of you and the baby," I continued running my hand on her tight belly. "Please."

As I waited on her answer, I looked at Miss Parade who was pouting in my car. There would be no way in hell I could let

Miss Daffany inside of the car with her. Miss Parade shook her head in disgust and looked at me and rolled her eyes. But what was I going to do? Ignore my friend when she needed my help?

I noticed a cab driving down the road and I flagged him down. And when I saw him pulling over, I reached in my pocket and grabbed some money. With the cab driver waiting, I gave the money to Miss Daffany. Then I took my house key off of the ring and handed it to her.

"Miss Daffany, take this and go to my place. I don't have to say I trust you, even though this drug has you, because you already know I do. So I'ma drop Miss Parade off and then we'll talk." She looked back at that skeezer and I redirected her attention toward me. "Miss Daffany, do you hear me? Go to my place and wait for me."

"O…Okay, I'll go," she said reluctantly.

I knew she didn't want to go but I needed to help her as best as I could. I know you think I'm a fool, and that it's impossible to change a dope, but I don't believe that. I believe if I flood Miss Daffany with enough love, it'll undue the curse her mother placed on her. As Miss Daffany entered the cab, I didn't take my eyes off of the car until she was through the light and out of sight. And then I turned to the bitch she called friend.

"Who the fuck are you?" I asked her.

"I'm somebody you can't get rid of simply by putting her in a cab. Me and Daffany are the same people. So unless you can understand that she loves get high just as much as I do, I suggest you get use to seeing my face, cause I ain't goin' nowhere. She makes me a lot of money and we work good together."

This bitch tried it. Didn't she know I could snatch her eyeballs out quicker than she could roll 'em? I was not about to sit here and watch her steal somebody I loved away from me. It just wasn't gonna happen. And I didn't care who had to get hurt in the process.

"Hear me and hear me good you, snaggle-tooth-little-

bitch! Now I don't know if you have anybody who cares about you, and to be honest, I don't give a fuck, but you're not about to interfere with me trying to get her cleaned up. And if I catch you around her again, smacking you in the face will be the least of your worries. I got a hammer for bitches like you and it's brand new and ain't been fired once. Give me a reason and you'll be the first."

"Whatever. You can have her," she said taking the pampers from the stroller she was pushing, placing them in the shopping cart. "But you should know Daffany is grown and in the end, it'll be her decision. Don't blame me."

With that she pushed the cart away. The ringing of the wheels rolling over the sidewalk faded as she walked further from me. I never committed murder, but if she didn't stay away from Daffany, I had a feeling she would be my first victim.

When I walked back to the car I noticed Miss Parade wasn't there. At first I thought she was leaned back in the seat and I couldn't see her. But the closer I got to the car, the more I realized she wasn't inside. She'd left. I don't understand why she hated me so much for helping our friend. And truthfully, I was starting not to care.

Parade

I couldn't believe Miss Wayne! The more he chose her over me the more I hated his guts and hers too. It was impossible to get a dope head off of drugs yet he insisted on trying. From here on out, if he wanted to fuck wit' her, then he wasn't fuckin' wit me. It's as simple as that.

"How much?" I asked the cab driver as we pulled up to my car in front of Jay's house. My heart ached when I saw Jay's car parked next to mine. I thought he was inside until I remembered we drove the motorcycle.

"Twelve dollars," he said reaching for my cash.

A part of me wanted to scratch his car up and break the windows. I hated the fact that he put me in such an awkward position. Why would he take me over his mother's house when he knew how she felt about me? After handing him my money, and watching him pull off, I eased toward my car. The moment I did, I heard the roar of Jay's motorcycle pulling behind me and my stomach fluttered. And just that quickly the hate I had for him diminished at the sight of him. But I would never let him know.

I walked fast enough to my car to look like I didn't want to be bothered, but slow enough for him to catch me if he hurried. Once at the passenger side, I threw my purse inside and walked toward the driver side, stalling. Jay immediately approached me.

"Parade," he yelled, his voice muffled under the helmet. "Wait up!"

"Jay, I'm not tryin' to hear this shit," I told him reaching for my car door. "Your mother got me fucked up and you do to." I opened my door and he slammed it shut. I leaned against the car with my arms crossed looking at him sideways. "What, Jay? What the fuck do you want? To take me back to your mom's so she can embarrass me some more?" He took off his helmet and placed it under his arm. And before speaking, he took two deep breaths.

"Did you just hit my mother back there?" He frowned and clenched his fist.

He asked me this question a hundred times already so I answered it by saying, "Yes I hit her!"

"Parade…you were out of pocket for that shit," he said stepping closer to me. I could tell he was torn and wanted to hurt me. "Way the fuck out!"

"Jay, please! " I put my hand in his face and he pushed it away. "She disrespected me and you let her. I told you I didn't want to go over there. Plus you knew she ain't like me. What were you tryin' to do, make me look like an idiot on purpose? Or wait…hold up…maybe I was your charity case."

He grabbed my wrist and threw them down. "Parade, I don't want to hear that shit you talkin' and don't try to turn shit around. I murdered people for less than what you did back there. You could've told me you were uncomfortable or that you wanted to leave. But you don't up and hit a nigga's moms!"

"Jay, fuck this shit! You always gettin' amusement at my expense and I'm tired of it. I have allowed you to use my body and my mind over and over again. And I'm changing and don't like the feeling of it anymore! It's a new day and I'm Parade Knight! Not your step stool or toilet!" I hadn't realized I was crying until I felt the warm liquid run down my face.

"Parade…you were wrong," he said softly. "You were wrong as shit."

"Tell me something you haven't said already." I just

wanted to get away from this embarrassing moment. "Otherwise let me go."

"Parade...," he said breathing heavily. "You were wrong...but I love you."

Did I hear him correctly?

"What?"

"I said...you were out of pocket for hittin' my mother, but I love you, Parade. I'm tired of playin' these games wit' you. And you gotta know I really do care about you after tonight. Had you been anybody else, we wouldn't even be speakin' face to face cuz I'd be talkin' to you over your grave," he said seriously.

"Jay, this is crazy and I'm not even sure how to handle it. I mean...everything is wrong right now. Everything! Why did you have to realize *now* that you want me? I'm engaged and I don't know what I'm gonna do plus I hit your mother's."

"Do you love him?" he managed getting off the topic of his mother for a moment.

"What?" I asked scratching my head and fiddling with my keys.

"I said do you love him?"

"Yeah...I mean no. I mean I think so Jay. I'm marryin' him ain't I? Why else would I walk down the aisle wit' him?" I turned my back toward him to enter my car.

I was almost in and then he walked up behind me, placed his helmet on the roof and wrapped his arms around me. I could feel his heartbeat as he held me. Without notice, for the second time tonight, tears fell down my eyes.

"I love you, Shawty," he said gripping me tighter. "I love you."

"I know. I can feel it," I answered truthfully.

"And I wanna be wit' you. I'm not sure how we goin' to do this, but we are. But you gotta apologize to my mom *first*."

"I know."

"And I'ma have her apologize to you but don't ever vio-

late like that again. I don't give a fuck how mad you get. That's my mother. And I'd say the same shit to her if she got out on you."

"I won't, Jay."

My body trembled in his arms. What was to become of my life when my heart belonged to him? I turned around and looked into his eyes. For the first time ever, I felt *genuine* love from a man. Wrapping my arms around his neck I kissed him. I didn't care about the details on how we would be one. I'd work everything out later. All that mattered was that he loved me, and I loved him too. At least for now.

Sweets

Sweets sat in a car across the street looking at Parade and Jay. Since she'd been there for over an hour, she saw they had gotten into a fight. It was apparent that they shared more than sex. It was obvious they were in love. With the information burning a whole in her head, she hoped she'd be able to use it to her advantage. Sitting back further in her seat to keep her disguise, she phoned the one person she knew would care.

"Smokes…it's me, Sweets," she said still watching Jay and Parade.

"What up?"

"Nothin'…just sittin' here watchin' your fiancé kiss Jay."

Silence.

"You sure it's them?" he asked breathing into the phone.

"Positive…I know what the fine ass nigga looks like," Sweets giggled. She quickly stopped when she realized she'd gone too far.

"Don't get fucked up," he told her. "Did she see you?"

"Nope…she too wrapped up to know I'm even here."

"Good…she'll get what she has comin' anyway, it's just a matter of time."

"Smokes," Sweets said slowly.

"What you want?"

"Uh…I want to know why you don't trust me. We don't even need her. I wish you'd just let me in on what you need her to do. I can do whatever she can for you but better. I love you

Smokes. I'm puttin' it all on the line for you, baby. Trust me," she pleaded sounding more like a pesky ass sales person.

Click.

"Smokes?" Sweets said looking at the phone.

Realizing she'd gone too far, she threw the phone in her passenger seat. Finally she understood that no matter what she did, she couldn't get through to him. But on her mother's life, she was still going to try.

Miss Wayne

I'm tired. Emotionally and physically. And all I want to do is come in, get Miss Daffany situated and get some rest. I have a big order of purses I got comin' in from some credit cards I got for my partner and have most of them sold already.

Walking up my stairs and toward my door, something didn't feel right. Maybe it was the fact that the door was halfway open. I was trying to see if I heard anything but the sound of my heart beating in my ears drowned out any noise. Finally at the door, I pushed it open and leaned up against the wall for support. My place was ransacked.

The couch pillows were thrown on the floor and the cabinets in the kitchen were open. With my hand on my heart, I tried to keep in some of the pain I felt inside. How could one of my closest friends betray me? How is this possible? I loved Miss Daffany!

I moved toward my bedroom already knowing she'd taken everything. Still I moved toward my closet, and toward a black jacket I kept in the back of it. I never wore it, just kept it there to stash some money. And sure nuff, everything was out. Including the purses I'd just bought for my clients. She wiped me clean.

I fell to the floor and cried. And when I did, I saw the keys on the bed I'd given Miss Daffany earlier. What hurt the most was not that she robbed me, was that my heart still believed she could change. I still believed that she could beat this thing.

But I could do nothing if she didn't believe it too.

"God…please help me. Please."

Parade

The next morning I stayed in bed for a few hours awake, before I even moved. Miss Wayne was on my mind and how we left each other bothered me. Daffany's addiction also ran through my head and I tried to push out the hate I had for her in my heart. And then there was, Jay. *Jay. Jay. Jay*. Just saying his name made me realize how much I loved him.

"What you thinkin' about, baby?" Smokes asked as he rubbed my flat stomach. "You look like you concentratin' on somethin and it ain't me," his voice deep and crumbly due to recently having woke up.

"Naw. Just thinkin' bout what I gotta do today," I lied looking away from him so he couldn't see my deceitful eyes.

"I wanna take you out today, you cool wit' that?"

I really wasn't cause Jay asked to see me today and I wanted to see him. I wanted to be with him. He told me he had somewhere special he wanted to take me, and if I could to pack a bag. It was amazing that since we reunited, we hadn't had sex once. And I was anxiously anticipating that moment.

"Actually I got somethin' to do, baby." I turned my head to look into his eyes. "Maybe we can do something tomorrow."

"Naw…we goin' out today. So whatever plans you got, drop 'em." His strokes ceased. And I sighed. Defeated and angry, a wave of hate overcame me.

"Baby…I wanna do that thing we do sometimes. You know, the thing I like but you hate."

"Smokes, you said I wouldn't have to do that again. We talked about it and you said it was a one time thing."

"So what…you don't want to please your nigga? Cause if you don't, anotha shawty will. I need a wifey who would be willing to do anything I say cause I say it. And if you can't be that, just give me the word and I'll find someone who can fill your shoes."

I didn't even know how to respond to that question mentally or physically. Technically I was still his fiancé, and the ring on my finger proved it. Or at least, that was the lie I had been telling myself. But I didn't want to be with him. I didn't love him. But he was dangerous, and mean and could lash out if he felt disrespected.

"You know I want to please you, baby. I'm thankful for everything you've done for me."

"That's what I wanted to hear," he said basking in his win. He moved over top of me, and straddled me. His thick hairy legs brushing against my waist. "Kiss it first, and get that shit hard. Put extra spit on it too cause you know I like it sloppy wet."

Taking one last look at him, I took his large dick out of his boxers and placed it in my mouth. My head game was still vicious so I'd hoped he'd be satisfied with that alone and not want to do the freaky shit he loved to do to me. It was degrading and made me feel like less than a person.

"Uh…that's it, baby, suck that shit!" His hands rested on the top of my head.

With his dick at full length, I got into it. I could feel his body shivering. "Aight…aight stop!" he said grabbing hold of his penis. "You tried to make me bust didn't you? You freaky little, bitch!" he said licking his lips. He paused for a second while he looked at me, and then I felt the warm liquid from his piss empty on my stomach. I turned my face to prevent any of his bodily fluid from getting into my mouth like last time. I was disgusted and angry all at once. But what could I do when this is

what he wanted? I didn't feel like I had a lot of options.

"You like that shit don't you, you little, bitch?" Urine continued to drain from his body.

I nodded yes while squinting my eyes.

"Tell me you like my piss all on your body."

"I like it all on my body." I responded dryly.

"Ahhhhhh...," he called out. Shortly after he jerked himself until his cloudy cum fell on my breasts.

I felt wet, used and unclean. Like a toilet. So I closed my eyes and thought about Jay. Hoping that I'd get to see him soon. And for a second...just one moment...nothing else seemed to matter.

"What do you think, baby?" I sat across from him at H20 on D.C.'s waterfront with a red long velvet box open in front of us. "You like it?"

"I love it," I picked up the bracelet and smiled. Trying to replace this morning's events from my head was proving to be difficult. Not to mention I was supposed to meet Jay in four hours at IHOP in Riverdale, Maryland even though Smokes told me to cancel my plans.

I was going to tell him that Miss Wayne's car was broken down and he needed my help. I'd say anything I could to be with Jay. For some reason, he was worth the risk. And earlier Jay sent me a text message requesting that I bring a bathing suit. Since I didn't want any problems with Smokes, I decided to buy one on the way. "It's beautiful," I continued eyeing the diamond bracelet in my hands. "What's the occasion?"

"Doesn't have to be an occasion, although I do want to know if you like your life with me?" He stared at me as if he were trying to see through me.

"I love my life with you, but uh...it's like, sometimes you change."

"It's not that I'm changing baby. It's just that I have a lot on my mind. And that's what I want to talk to you about." He wiped his head with a napkin from the table.

"Okay…I'm listening."

He looked around and waited for a few people who were going to their table to sit down. When he was sure they weren't listening, he said, "I need you to help out with the business a little, baby. I wouldn't ask you accept I can't trust anybody else right now. Niggas is turnin' on me and that nigga Zeeway's a punk to this kind of shit. It's got to be you."

"The business?" I repeated leaning in. I mean, what did I know about the business?

"Yes…you not a fool so I know you know what I do for a living. I wouldn't be able to afford this lifestyle without hustling. And lately I been feelin' like I ain't got no help, so I'ma need you to get rid of some of that load. Can you do that for me?"

"It depends."

"It depends?" His face was distorted.

"Yes…it depends on what you want me to do, baby. I mean…I don't know nothin' about what you do." I looked around to be sure no one else could hear me. "I would probably make things worse for you, and I wouldn't want to do that either."

"So I take care of you, give you the world, spare your life and you act ungrateful?"

Spare me life? I thought. That comment scared me.

"No, baby…I don't mean to be ungrateful, it's just that, I don't want to get involved. That lifestyle is not me. I'm a fighter not a hustler."

Silence filled the space between us and I could feel him mentally pushing me backwards. Why would he ask me to risk my life?

"Parade…if you don't think you can do what it takes, this relationship is over."

Normally I'd be upset, but for some reason, I felt a weight lift off of my shoulders. He had given me the excuse I needed to be with Jay. After the piss thing earlier, I had expected to think of the best lie to excuse my betrayal, to be with my true love and here he was, giving me an easy way out. I knew if I didn't take it now, I'd never get the choice again.

"I understand." I placed the bracelet back in the box and slid it toward him. "If you give me a few days, I'll get my things and leave." I attempted to ease the ring off of my finger too but he looked at me coldly, I guess not expecting my response. So I kept the ring on. He didn't speak till it was securely back on my finger.

"You think it's that easy huh?" he asked me evilly.

"What you mean?"

"I know about your little boyfriend Jay," he said in a low voice. "And there's no way in hell I'm gonna just let you be with that nigga. Not while I'm alive anyway. Besides, you gonna be my future wife."

"I don't know what you're talking about." Sweat formed on my forehead. How did he know? "I haven't been wit Jay since before I got wit you." I don't know why I continued to lie but I couldn't stop.

"Bitch, you gonna sit over there and keep lyin' to me? Or do you want me to have somebody take care of him and see if you can still stick to that bullshit. He can be dead in five minutes. You want me to make the call? You want me to cause his mother and the rest of his family to have to plan that man's funeral? Huh?"

Who was he? Everything about him had changed at it appeared to have happened overnight. Instead of saying anything else, I remained silent.

"Now…you're gonna do what I need you to do. Now I let you fuck main man and neva said nothin'. You thought you were foolin' somebody but I knew all along. But that shit stops here.

You my bitch and you belong to me. You don't do shit without me."

Wow, I'd been sleeping with the devil all this time but never knew. But how could I not? He killed one of my best friends.

"You ready to hear what I got to say now?"

I remained silent because I was speechless. There were no words to express the thoughts which ran through my mind. So I remained quiet and listened.

Miss Wayne

It took me a few hours to clean my place. I guess I was trying to find a way to get over everything by staying busy. Taking two bags full of trash outside, I was shocked when I saw Keith standing in the hallway. I didn't realize how much I missed him until I saw his face. And most of all, after everything Miss Daffany put me through; I just needed somebody to talk too. And a part of me was starting to believe he never did the things Miss Daffany said he did. But my doubt felt more like betrayal.

Instead of telling him how much I needed him, I said, "What the fuck you doin' here, Keith?"

Pushing past him I made my way to the steps and toward the dumpster outside. A guy I fucked a few months back when Keith was tripping nodded at me. I nodded back. Keith was right on my trail, sniffin' behind this delicious piece of ass like he always did.

"Baby, can we talk?" he asked, as he followed me after I dumped my garbage and headed back to my place. "I miss you and you know I'd never do anything to hurt you." I jotted up the steps in silence not knowing what to say. His voice alone had me wanting to throw my arms around him.

"I don't want to talk, Keith. You violated me *and* my trust. And I could never go back to that again." I walked inside and flopped on the couch.

Dropping to his knees he said, "Baby, I'd never violate your trust. As a matter of fact, I came to your crib yesterday to

talk to you and caught Daffany roaming through your shit."

I was stunned.

"What are you talking about?"

"I came by and she was throwing stuff around trying to find something. I knew you wasn't there because your car wasn't outside. Eventually she walked to the back and came out the door. She had your money in her hands. I caught her at the door right before she took off. I even got your cash back." He handed me a wad of cash.

"You saw Miss Daffany?" I asked, taking my money back. "When she was here?"

"Yeah, baby… I stopped her and questioned her, and found out she was stealing from you. She's fucked up .You can't fuck wit her no more. I see a lot of that shit in my line of work. All she's gonna do is bring you down. The only thing she cares about is dope! I been tryin' to tell you not to fuck wit that bitch."

My head fell in shame.

"Well if you were here, and you cared so much, why didn't you close my door?"

"I'm sorry," he said. "I was so caught up in making sure she got out of your building that when I put her out, I didn't go back. I'm sorry about that. I guess her fuckin' over your messed me up. And I tried to reach you but you wouldn't accept my calls. But let's not do this anymore. You know you're the love of my life."

"So, you actually saw her stealing from me," I said softly. I couldn't move past Miss Daffany's deceit.

"Yes," he repeated. I guess I wanted him to say something different than what he had already. "Like I said, you wouldn't answer my calls. I'm sorry, Wayne."

He was right, ever since I suspected him to be a liar, I had been ignoring his calls, but now here he was coming to my rescue.

"Can I take you out?" he asked rubbing my knee. "And

show you how much you mean to me?"

I nodded yes.

I got myself together preparing to go out. I made up my mind that I was not going to accept any more of Miss Daffany's calls unless the Lord Himself came down here and begged me. I just hoped I could do it.

Daffany

The brick wall I was leaning against woke me because it was cold against my skin and the mattress under my body was damp. Looking around I knew I was in an alley in Southeast D.C., and I tried to find somebody familiar. I remember coming here last night after copping about two hundred dollars worth of dope. The alley was the place we came to smoke amongst our own-other dopeheads. And I'd been here so much I could almost call this place home. It was the only place consistent.

"You up already?" Carmen asked. She was laying on the mattress on my right. I was startled because I didn't see her at first.

"Yeah…what happened last night?" I asked rubbing my belly. My baby would move first thing in the morning and it was the only time I remembered or cared that I was pregnant.

"What didn't happen?" Carmen asked as she sat up next to me. "We made a lot of money last night and spent it up."

"We?" I repeated. Lately it seemed like she was pimping me. She had a knack of finding the freakiest and nastiest men on earth for me to deal with. "Cause it seems like I been doin' all the work. You might suck a few dicks, but for real, all the dope we buy is compliments of me." I told her stroking my tummy. The baby was kicking a lot and I figured it was hungry. I had to feed it even though I didn't want food.

"I do just as much shit as you do," Carmen said standing up, brushing the back of her dingy jeans. "Now come on, we got

to be somewhere at 10:00. The man's wife leaves for work and he gonna give us $100.00 dollars if he gets wit' you."

"Us? If I'm doing all the work how come he gonna give *us* some money? That's what I'm talking about. I'm not feeling this shit no more, Carmen." I stood up and pulled my blue YMCA T-shirt down so that it fell over the back of my jeans.

"He gonna give *us* the money cause I get *you* the business," she said rubbing her arms. "Without me you wouldn't be shit! Now let's go!" She walked up the block."

As I walked behind her, I started feeling like I didn't need her. After all, it was my pussy that was getting all of the dope we used so what *was* her purpose?

"Carmen, I think I"ma go off on my own. That way I can save up more money and get a place for me and my baby."

"Oh really?" She turned around and placed her hands on her hips. "So where you gonna start, Daffany? You don't know nobody sep' them cheap ass hustlers around the Manor. Plus, I can have somebody kick your ass everyday for a week if you try to back out on me now. Then you wouldn't have to worry about your baby."

"What?" I was shocked at her response.

"You heard me. If you try to act like you're a solo act I'll have somebody kick your ass everyday of the week."

I was fuming! She got me fucked up if she thought she was gonna to get to me like that. I knew for a fact I was tougher than her.

"Oh really?" I said stepping up to her with my fist balled up. "Why don't you try it now! Why you gotta have somebody else do your dirty work. Man up, bitch! Fight me straight up!"

Dopeheads started looking at us and I could tell they were prepared for some excitement to help get their minds off of their fucked up lives. Instead of doing anything, she backed down. Just like I thought. She was a punk!

"You know what, fuck you! If you think you can get the

kind of money I find us, be gone! But don't come crying to me when it ain't working," she said walking away. "My pussy is doin' me just fine!"

The moment the words left her mouth I knew I made a major mistake. I didn't have a friend in the world and if I let her go, I wouldn't even have an enemy. Everything in me felt that if I had another chance with Miss Wayne, I would surely take it. Or at least I'd try. I'm sure by now Keith told a bunch of lies on me. All I wanted to do the day I went to Miss Wayne's was get some rest, and clean up. But when I turned the key to the door, Keith came up behind me in the hallway.

"What you doin' here, bitch?" he said. "I should fuck you up right now for the problems you caused!" he continued pressing his weight on my back so that my tummy pressed firmly against Miss Wayne's door.

"Please don't hurt me," I pleaded. I hoped someone would come to my rescue. It seemed as if lately, the most violent things were occurring in my life. "I'll leave and never come back I promise."

He grabbed a fist full of my hair and mushed my face against the cold door. I could taste my own blood from my teeth pressing against my lips, while my baby kicked wildly.

"Listen…I want you to stay the fuck away from here, and never come back. If you do come back I'll kill you with my bare hands. You hear me?"

"Yes," I said shaking my head. Tears ran down my face. "I won't come back. Just please don't hurt me."

"And if you tell Wayne anything I'll find you. Trust me."

He released me and I left, vowing to never see my friend again. But now, here with Carmen, all I thought about was getting clean and taking care of my baby. Miss Wayne's home was just what we needed to get ourselves together. But I had fucked

up so much there was not turning back.

"Carmen," I called out before she left me too.

She turned around and said, "What?"

"I'm sorry." My head dropped. "You're right; I can't do this on my own."

She walked back up to me and smiled slyly. "Okay, but you betta remember next time that although the pussy belong to you, its cause of me you gettin' paid for it."

And just like that, I was right back where I started. In hell.

T. STYLES

Parade

I saw Jay's headlights approach my car and I smiled. Then I quickly looked at myself in the mirror and swallowed the Ciroc vodka, straight up that I had in my cup. I wasn't able to leave Smokes yesterday but I made sure nothing would stop me from seeing my baby tonight. I needed a break after the shit Smokes ran down to me, and spending time with Jay was perfect. Like he asked me to, the only thing I brought with me was a black bathing suit with rhinestones throughout it. I had also taken my tracks out and wore my natural hair down. With my new shoulder length mane, I had it styled in a cute little bob that brushed my cheeks and I hoped Jay would like it.

"You ready?" he asked me as he opened my car door. He smelled and looked so sexy I wanted him right here. We met in Arundel Mills, parking lot in Maryland.

"Yeah I'm ready, baby." I wished I had a little more to drink when exiting the car. For some reason I was nervous. It was like it was the first time we'd gotten together. "I been waiting for this all night."

When I slid into his 2008 silver Tahoe my body melted within the leather seats. I loved the smell of a brand new car mixed with men's cologne. He kept looking at me from the corner of his eyes and I tried my best to keep my tummy sucked in, and my hair neat.

"You look sexy," he told me maneuvering on the roads. "I'm feelin' that haircut."

"Thank you." I fondled with my hair again unconsciously.

"Why do you do that?" He turned up the music lightly.

"Do what?"

"Fidget wit' yourself every time you wit me?" He paused. "I said you look good, Parade, ain't no need in feelin' uncomfortable. I want you to relax when you're around me."

"I am…but…I don't want you to get turned off either. I know what kind of girls you're use to."

"Parade, unlearn all of that shit you think about me." He rubbed his hand on my knee. "I want you to see I'm real wit' you. And I'm not the same stupid ass nigga who put you through that shit when we were together. But it ain't gonna mean shit if you don't believe me."

This whole thing is crazy to me. Back in the day he wasn't feelin' me, now he was doing all he could to prove he *was* feelin' me. How come it took droppin' his ass to get my respect? When I gave him my heart and my body he stomped on it. And as much as I wanted to believe he had changed, so much damage had been done to my self esteem.

"Can I ask you somethin'?" I said changing the subject slightly.

"Anything," he said smoothly.

"Have you ever asked Sky to do anything illegal for you? You know…to help you get money?" I was out of line for asking him but I needed to know. My heart had already chosen Jay, but my mind still was locked on Smokes. And I wanted to know if he had been playing me all along or if he ever cared about me.

"You playin' right?" he asked pulling over on the side of the road. "Please don't tell me this nigga askin' you to get involved in his shit." I didn't respond. "I knew it!"

"You knew what?"

As if he was holding something from me he cleared his throat and said, "Why you ask me that?"

"I'm just askin', Jay. It's not that serious."

"Listen…if that nigga askin' you to get involved in his shit I'll kill that nigga."

That turned me on.

"No, Jay…he wouldn't do that." I lied. "I'm just asking you hypothetically."

"Hypothetically huh?" He was silent before he said, "Parade…I don't think that nigga's in your corner. And I think you need to be careful."

"Why you say that?"

"Remember the dude Zeeway?" I nodded. "Well the way he talks about the shit Smokes do behind your back, I can tell he ain't got no intentions on being serious about you. If anything…he's been checkin' a lot for that shorty he run wit all the time."

He must've been talking about Sweets.

"Jay, please," I said smacking my lips. "Don't act like you were the most faithful-ess nigga when you were dealin' wit Sky. And for your information I'm sure that nigga cheats so you wastin' your breath tellin' me somethin' I already know. I haven't met a man on earth who can be faithful. So why should mine be any different? And look at me!" I said realizing I was cheating to. "Look at us!"

"So that's okay with you? To marry a nigga you know ain't shit? It's one thing to fuck wit somebody like that but to be with him for the rest of your life is stupid, Parade!"

"I'm here with you ain't I?"

"And what's that's supposed to mean?"

"It means that I know you got somebody somewhere, Jay. So I'm ridin' this shit out until the wheels fall off. I'm a big girl now so I won't cry if you cut me off later. You hurt me enough for a lifetime."

He sighed.

"I know niggas cheat and I'm not even entertaining that

bullshit you just said about me. Yeah I got a few bitches I fuck from time to time, but I'd cut them all off the minute you stop playin' house wit that punk ass nigga at home." I looked at him and rolled my eyes. "Now I'm not tryin' to argue with you. What I'm sayin' is this," he exhaled. "He talk about shit like you not even in the picture. Like marrying you was always a joke. Parade, I don't think dude *ever* had any intentions on marryin' you."

"You just runnin' your mouth." I was growing irritated. I hated hearing what I already suspected. "He had me pick out a wedding gown and everything."

"Play the tapes back in your head. Did he ever give you a date for the wedding?" I was silent as I thought about his question. And as much as I hated to admit it, Jay was right. He never gave me a date and I never asked for fear of making him angry. "You playin' yaself!"

"You know what, Jay…fuck this shit!" I said as I exited his car. I walked quickly on the road ahead of me. Why couldn't I fall for someone who loved me? Instead I fell for Smokes, a user, a murderer and a cheat. I wished Jay would've came back in my life before Smokes but after he realized how wrong he was for treating me badly back in the day.

"Parade," Jay said running up behind me. The truck lights behind us shined bright. "Stop doin' this bullshit. Stop fuckin' runnin!"

I don't know what it is. Every time things get emotional between me and Jay, I run away. I think it's my way of preparing for the day he realizes he really doesn't want me. I guess I want to be the one to end it first.

"Jay, please!" I tried pushing him off. "Just let me be!"

He stopped holding me against my will and said, "You know what, I'm sick of this shit. If you want to keep runnin' away from me than do it. I'm not putting up with this shit no more. Anything I say to you, you turn around and I'm sick of it.

All I was doing was trying to protect you. That's it."

I could tell in his voice I was about to lose him so I turned around.

"Jay…uh….I."

"You ain't gotta say nothin' baby," he told me looking in my eyes. "Just stop running away from me. And we ain't got to talk about dude because I already know what type of time he's on. But do this…when you go home tell him you want to marry him *now* and that you don't care about having a wedding. I guarantee you that nigga gonna give you an excuse on why he can't do it," he continued as he grabbed my hand and walked me back to the car.

"Why do you think you know so much?" I asked sitting in my seat. He started up the ignition.

"Cause I know niggas and I know game. And you gotta always be thinkin' two steps ahead." I thought about what he said long and hard and I took his words to heart. "But tonight let's not think about that shit. Cause you wit me."

He was right. I was all his.

Smokes

Smokes was sitting in his house watching his kid run around the kitchen. He was waiting for his mother to pick him up because being around a busy three year old wasn't something he was trying to do right now.

"So what's the hold up?" Ace, his Dominican connect asked over the phone. "We waited long enough."

"I know, but I'm gettin' ready to move on it now. You gotta give me some time."

"Well you ain't got no more time" he reminded him. "I'm sure you dry out there by now."

Ace was right, unless he got Parade to get on that plane he wouldn't be able to run his business. Ace was instrumental. Not only did he supply him with the best dope to keep his operation running smoothly, he gave it to him at a good price. All Smokes had to do was convince naive unsuspecting woman to make the trip to the Dominican Republic. Once there, they'd be sold into sex slavery. Smokes had been involved in this line of business for the past ten years. American women were exotic over there and went for much more.

"She'll be there," Smokes said seriously. "If I have to bring her there myself.

"That's what I wanted to hear."

When Smokes hung up on him, he called Zeeway. Ever since he'd been home, he'd been using him to handle all of his

dirty work. And tonight he wanted to talk to him about another job.

"Zeeway, make your way over here. And quick. We have a lot to discuss."

"I'm on my way now."

Parade

The longer we drove to our destination, the more beautiful things became. Jay had taken me to a gorgeous rental home in Deep Creek, Maryland. I never knew Maryland had places like this. The mountains were large and sat in the backdrop like a beautiful painting. And when we entered the cabin style house, it had a smooth country appeal. It was far more relaxing than anything I'd been around in my entire life.

"Sit down at the kitchen table, baby," he said as he ran back to the car returning with four bags. When I tried to help him he refused so I sat down and my legs shook nervously.

"Just relax and let me do this." He unpacked all of the bags alone.

"Why are you doing all of this, Jay? I'm not use to you treating me like this and I don't know how to handle it."

"I'm doing this because I was wrong for how I treated you." He gazed into my eyes. "So tonight don't ask why, just go with the flow. Aight?"

I nodded yes.

"I got you," he winked. "So put on that bathing suit you brought and meet me on the balcony."

"The balcony?"

"Just do it," he demanded. "it's back there."

I disappeared into the rental home stealing a look at the scenery. I was comfortable and couldn't wait to see what he had

in store. Once in the bathroom, I slid into my black bathing suit with silver rhinestones and looked at myself in the mirror. I liked what I saw so I smiled. For the first time in a long time I felt comfortable and sexy. I wasn't sure if it was the buzz I had going or anxiousness. I ran my hand through my bob style haircut, and struck a pose.

"I'm gonna make him realize how much he needs me tonight," I said to myself.

Sliding into my black high heels, I seductively walked to the balcony. My mouth dropped when I saw the Jacuzzi running with rose pedals moving throughout. On the side was a bottle of Ace of Spades champagne chilling in a silver ice bucket. It was dark but I could still see the leaves on the trees moving in the warm breeze. This was the most romantic thing he'd ever done for me.

"Damn, Parade," he said looking at my body. "You're sexy as shit! I must've been trippin' when I let you go."

Hearing him say that made me feel warm inside. Kicking my shoes off, I exposed my manicured feet and slowly eased into the water. The bubbles tickled my body. Then I moved in front of him and wrapped my arms around his neck. His curly hair was wet and clinged to his scalp. Jay was the finest man I'd ever seen in my life. And tonight he was all mine.

"You're fine as hell," I told him pressing my body against his.

"You know you gonna be mine right?" he asked me as our bodies floated underneath us.

I remained silent.

"I'm not gonna play this game long with you and dude, but after everything I put you through." He continued. "I know you gotta find out on your own what type of nigga he is first. And I'm willing to work at it Parade, but I ain't gonna wait forever. Pretty soon you gonna have to make a decision on who you want. Me or him…straight up."

Instead of speaking I just pressed my lips against his. Everything about right now felt good. It felt right and I didn't want to spoil it with verbal details. When I felt his fingers running over my body my heart raced in anticipation of being with him again. Sexually and mentally.

"I want you," I said kissing him passionately. "Now."

When I said that I felt him move the seat of my bathing suit over and ease into me slowly. The water pushing us softly didn't take away from how he felt. Ummmmmm. My mouth remained open until he pushed everything he had into my wetness. The water bubbles danced around us.

"Damn you feel so fuckin' good, Parade!" He held my waist. "I miss this shit."

"You too, baby. You feel so good."

I slowly began to wind my hips in small circles. My stomach felt tingly as he remained in control of my waist and met my pumps with each motion I made. The last time I had sex with Jay, he was cold and heartless. Now it was passionate and sweet. Removing my breasts from my bathing suit he sucked my nipples softly. I bit my bottom lip as the warmth from his tongue circled my nipples. They immediately hardened in his mouth. In all of the times we've been together, Jay has never sucked my breasts. And he was so damn good at it.

"Don't stop, Jay…please!"

"I ain't gonna stop hittin' this shit until you remember the nigga I am. You mine, Parade Knight. You my, lady."

In and out. Over and over, Jay consistently hit the right spots. Although the lovemaking was on point, for some reason I wanted more. And since he was working overtime to show me he was a changed man, I knew it would be on me to spice things up.

"Jay, stop bullshittin' and fuck this pussy!"

He looked at me like he finally saw me for the first time. And with his eyes, he agreed with me. But what he did next I didn't expect. He lifted me out of the water and sat me on the edge

of the Jacuzzi. I was a little chilly at first until he moved my bathing suit aside and ran his tongue around my clit.

In my entire life, no man had ever eaten my pussy and I didn't realize how good it felt. I heard people talk about it, but never knew it would feel this good. Every part of me was sensitive as he sucked on my throbbing clitoris. I couldn't hold back. I grabbed the back of his head and unconsciously pushed my wetness toward his face. His tongue strokes didn't stop until he sucked ever last drop of my oil. My body shivered as I looked at him.

"Oh my, gawd!"

He gently pulled me back into the water and said, "I'm not done with you yet. "I'm about to fuck this pussy up!" He began going in and out of me roughly. The oily residue from my last climax allowed him to enter me with extreme ease. "I'ma leave my mark on this pussy."

My entire body tingled from my toes to nipples. I was open, and knew it. There was no way I could go on with marrying Smokes or living with him for that matter. I wanted out. But what was I gonna do? I knew first hand the kind of man he could be. After all, he had my best friend Sky killed and promised to kill Jay if I saw him again. All I knew was this, if I had to lay down my life to be with Jay, then it was a chance I was willing to take. Cause living without him anymore, would already make me want to die.

Daffany

I need to stop this shit but I don't know how. Nothing about my life makes sense anymore and I don't know what to do. And I can't call the one person I know cares about me because I messed up.

"You're beautiful," the trick said as I lay in his bed, with him on top of me. His wife was at work. I waited in his basement for two hours in the dark, and the moment she hit the door, he snuck me upstairs. On my way up, I noticed family pictures dressed the walls. His family was beautiful and still he wasn't satisfied. What I wouldn't give for a life like this. "I didn't know you were so beautiful."

I smiled. I would give him credit for being nicer than most tricks but I didn't understand his reason. I felt like I didn't deserve such kindness. I was a whore and whores are supposed to be used. Still I couldn't get over how handsome he was. More handsome than I would think a trick would be. I mean, he could get anybody he wanted, so why me? His light brown eyes and honey brown skin was perfect, and his build was muscular, sexy and he smelled good.

Rubbing his hands on my face, he looked deeply into my eyes. This was weird but his touch caused me to melt. The only thing that fucked this moment up was the smell of the condom. It made me nauseous at first. Certain smells irritated me. Pushing the scent out of my mind, I imagined this was my home, and that I was carrying his baby. I even tried to push out of my mind that

he had a fetish for pregnant woman who were showing. He said something about our pussies being tigher the further along in the pregnancy we were. And since I couldn't fuck myself, I had no idea if it was true or not, so I took his word for it.

Easing into my body, he sucked on my bottom lip lightly. He was making love to me and it felt so good. I knew what this was all about. Money. Still, I decided to enjoy myself. I needed his attention right now. I needed to feel like a lady, even if the man on top of me was not mine. A light smile spread across my face until he bit my lip so hard my body tensed up and I screamed in his face.

"Shut the fuck up, bitch!" he stole me in my jaw. "You know you like this shit don't you!" He hit me with a closed fist again. "Whores like you love this kind of shit and you ain't no different!"

I saw my blood fall on his lip and he wiped it off. Where am I? What's going on? Who is this man on top of me? When I looked up at him, I remembered that he had just hit me. He stole me so hard, that for a brief moment, I lost memory.

"I'm sorry," he said softly lightly touching my face again seeing my tears. His strokes harder and harder inside of me. It was like he was getting off on what he was doing. He went from crazy to nice instantly. "I didn't mean to hit you so hard. Are you okay?"

Tasting my own blood and feeling my baby kick wildly I still managed to lie. All I wanted was to get out of this house safely along with my money. Because after this, I was gonna have to get high. And if God helped me just this one time, I promised myself that I'd never get in this position again. Fear set in when I realized I'd made many promises to the Lord and kept none of them.

"I'm fine." He continued to rape me. "I'm okay, really. I just got to go home."

"Good. I'm glad you're okay." He rubbed my face again

before his hands found their way on my throat. He squeezed and squeezed some more.

As he choked me I tried my best to fight him, my baby too. We were both fighting for our lives. Not being able to breathe was petrifying. He continued to rape me while he prevented oxygen from entering my body. And then I felt light. I felt this feeling before when I had my own apartment and someone I trusted broke in. No longer able to defend myself, I gave in to the feeling. Sure I'd been in the worst kind of trouble since fucking with heroin, but this was different. I wanted to die. I wanted to leave the hell I lived in daily. I welcomed death with open arms. Tell Miss Wayne and Parade I love them. Please.

When I felt water on my face I thought I was dreaming until I could feel him going in and out of me. I'm still here? I'm still alive? I had hoped he wouldn't torture me anymore. I had hoped he'd be done and I'd be in heaven but I wasn't.

"That's right, beautiful, get up. I'm not half done with you yet." He said licking his lips. "I'ma get my full moneys worth from your beautiful whore ass. I love fuckin' whores like you. You shouldn't be walking around passing out good pussy. Somebody got to take it. Somebody got to put you in your place. That's my job."

"Please let me go," I cried. "Please…I just want to go home." Without waiting he hit me so hard in the face, I felt my skull move. This was the scariest situation I had ever been in, in my life and I didn't see a way out. For the next few hours, he continuously choked me and brought me back to consciousness. And each time, I hoped I wouldn't wake up but every time I did.

Miss Wayne

Getting back with me was not going to be easy. I made up in my mind that I was gonna send his ass through hurdles before he finally got a piece of this boy-band-ass again. And trust me, he was certainly fighting for it.

I was in the Saks Fifth Outlet in Arundel Mills mall trying out a cute pair of black pants. Keith was taking me out and I wanted to make sure I dried his pockets up starting with a shopping spree. Everything was going okay until I tried to ease into the size ten pair of pants I was trying on. With one leg in, and the other out, I leaned up against the mirror to slide my right leg into the other side. Then I stood on two feet and became frustrated because the pants wouldn't come past my knees.

"Excuse me, miss," I said calling out to the lady who was helping me at the store. I waited impatiently for her to respond.

"Yes?" she called out nicely. "You need anything, sir?"

"I thought I asked you for a size ten? These don't fit so they clearly are not what I asked you for."

"Sir…I did get the size ten like you asked. Did you want to try a few sizes up?"

"Did I ask you to give me a pair a few sizes up?" I said sarcastically placing my hands on my hips.

Silence.

"No sir." Her attitude was nonchalant. "Did you want me to give you another pair?"

"Yes! And hurry up!"

"Are you okay, baby? Do you want me to find another size?" Keith asked in the background.

"The only thing I want you to do is get your wallet ready."

I waited for five minutes and she still hadn't brought them to me. This bitch was bout to make me go off. I know damn well these ain't no size ten and I don't care what she says. And to prove it, I decided to take them off to check the tag. *Damn.* They are a size 10. I wasn't trippin' though cause as far as I was concerned, someone had tagged them incorrectly. I always wore a size ten and I knew my body. Maybe I didn't hold my stomach tight enough.

I tried to wiggle into them again. But when I did, the entire pants burst open on the sides. My legs looked like a scene from Incredible Hulk in the pants.

"Here you go, sir."I took off the torn pants and accepted the new pair.

"Thanks, honey. You can take these back. They didn't fit because ya'll had em tagged wrong." I handed her the defective merchandise over the dressing room door.

"Sir, you'll have to pay for these," she told me taking the torn material from me.

"I'm not paying for ya'lls error. Had they been tagged correctly it would not have happened. I know what size I wear, sweetheart."

After taking the other pants from her I tried them on and the same thing happen. They tore once they got around my thighs. Fuck it! I'll go somewhere else since it's obvious they use cheap ass material here. It's a waste of my time. After I got dressed I grabbed my purse and rolled my eyes at the clerk when I walked past her.

"Your cheap material is hanging on the back of the door."

"Bitch!" she said under her breath as I walked past her.

"Your wretched ass mother," I told her back as I looked

back.

They needed to learn how to treat paying customers around here and I didn't have the time to teach 'em. I strutted past her and toward the door. I could see her in my peripheral vision having a hissy fit. She could waste her time, but not mine.

"You okay, honey?" Keith asked me holding my bags as we left the store. I had put a dent in the mall already and figured it was time for us to leave anyway.

"I'm fine." I told him still trying to get Miss Daffany out of my mind. For some reason, today I thought about her even more and I was sure I was lashing out on everyone. "Just a little hungry that's all."

Right when I said that, my cell phone rang. I didn't recognize the number but had a feeling it was somebody wanting a purse. I had just got my hands on Gucci's spring collection and knew they'd be eatin' them up the moment the word got out. Everybody knew I had the best prices in town.

"Sing to me," I told the caller as I switched my way down the mall.

"Miss Wayne," a voice called out lightly. My heart dropped along with my purse. I knew it was Miss Daffany.

"Miss Daffany…is that you?" I picked my purse up off the floor.

"I n…need your…help," she stuttered. "I'm hurt real bad."

"Baby, don't get involved in that shit," Keith whispered. "She got to find her way on her own."

"Miss Daffany…I…I don't know," I looked at him. "You really hurt my feelings the way you left last time. And I don't know if I could put myself through that again. I'm sorry."

"Miss Wayne, please." She sobbed. "I need you. I'm ready to change. I'm ready to start over. I'm scared for me and my baby."

I looked at Keith and than away from him. There was no

way I could allow her to be out there alone even if that meant *me* being alone.

"But you stole from me, Daffany. You took from me what I would've gladly given if you would've just asked."

"Steal from you?" she repeated. "On my life I never too anything from you!"

"She's lying," he interjected. "Now don't get caught up in her shit no more. She's using you and this shit is not going to stop. Now what do you want to do?"

"Miss Wayne, I don't know what he told you, but it's all a lie. I need you now more than anything that I would never take from you." She paused. "Now today I killed somebody."

"What?!" I screamed startling a few passing people.

"Yes. With a letter opener. He tried to kill me and I'm ready to change now. I've learned my lesson, Miss Wayne."

Chills ran through my body after her hearing her statement.

"Just tell me where you are and I'm on my way."

After I got the information from her, I placed my phone in my purse and looked at Keith. I knew he would be angry but what did he want me to do? Abandon my family? Plus she commited the ultimate crime to save herself. She needed me now more than ever.

"If you go get her, it's over between you and I. I'm serious this time. No more running back to me."

I burst into laughter right in his face.

"Nigga it's *been* over between you and I. And if you ever cared about me, you would've never asked me to choose between you and my friends. Have a nice life," I continued walking away. "And thanks for the shopping spree."

It hurt leaving him. But niggas came a dime a dozen while true friends came once in a lifetime.

Parade

I told myself I was stopping by to see Jay but I knew I wasn't. I was really coming by to visit my mother. I hadn't laid eyes on her since I left and since they lived in the same complex, something in me told me to try. In the past I'd ask Miss Wayne if he'd seen her, but he was too busy chasing behind Daffany when he was around the way to notice.

As I walked through my old hallway, the familiar feeling of despair, hurt and pain overwhelmed me. When I lived here I was nothing but black and ugly Parade Knight. I wasn't a girl that people liked. Nobody really fucked with me outside of my friends. And I wasn't entirely sure that things had changed.

Once at my mother's place, I could feel my heart pounding. Preparing to knock, I stopped moments before my knuckles and the door made contact. *What am I doing here?* My mother hates me and my father could care less if I'm dead or alive. Turning to walk away, I decided to go home and face life with my crazed fiancé, while I waited on the love of my life to call. And then *he* walked out.

"Parade?" my father's voice trailed behind me.

I stopped in my steps taking in his deep voice. Slowly I turned around to face him. Although the salt outweighed the pepper color in his hair now, he was still handsome. And his Nestle chocolate colored beautiful. I always thought our complexion

look better on him than it ever did on me. The only thing that was different was his eyes. They looked heavy, like he hadn't been getting much sleep. I knew he was on his way to work because he wore the same blue uniform he always did, and carried a brown paper bag filled with his lunch.

"Hey, daddy," I said walking up to him. "How have you been?"

My tone was even because I didn't know what to expect. My father worked eighteen hour days and was hardly ever home when I lived here. And when he was home, he was sleep. That's why we never had the relationship a daughter and father should have. The only memories I had of my father were of his smelly work boots, the sweat of his uniform and the fact that he loved my fried chicken. He wasn't there to witness the verbal abuse my mother placed on me. And when he was, he appeared to ignore it.

"Parade…where have you been?" he said in a concerned tone. His voice quivered as I watched his lunch bag fall to the filthy hallway floor. "I have been so worried about you. It's been over a year."

Without waiting, he grabbed my body and held me closely. I wept in his arms. In all of my years, my father never held me. He never seemed to care. And now, here he was embracing me strongly. I didn't mind the sweaty smell of his construction uniform. His 6'4 inch frame covered and soothed me like one of Miss Wayne's warm blankets. For the first time I felt at home in his arms.

"Daddy, how have you been?" I said wiping my tears and reluctantly pulling away from him. "You look so good," I continued picking his lunch up off the ground, handing it to him.

"I been fine, sweetheart." He appeared shocked to see me. "Why haven't you called? It's been so long. And whenever I'd ask the Wayne boy, or Daffany about you, they'd say you were fine."

"I am, Daddy." I gave him a light smile. "Just needed to get away that's all."

"I understand. I guess…but I've ben so worried." A loud horn sounded outside and he glanced at his watch. "Well, honey, I have to go to work now. But I want you to come around more often. Please…I really miss you."

I hugged him again and said, "I will, Daddy."

Taking one last look at me, he rushed down the stairs where his friend for years was waiting for him in a blue construction van.

"And, Parade," he said before exiting the door. "Speak to your mother. She might not say it, but she's been worried about you too." With that he was gone.

With the door still cracked, I walked into the apartment I'd lived in for years when I was a child. Nothing had changed much. She still had the same drab cream furniture in the living room, and African art decorations on the wall. Africa was showcased everywhere yet I found no sense of pride for myself. She was in the kitchen washing the dishes when I walked up behind her.

"Mama."

She stopped what she was doing, and slowly turned around. When her eyes met mine, she smiled. It was the first time my mother looked at me like she was happy to see my face. And then like a light switch had been flicked off, her entire mood changed.

"What are you doing here?" she asked washing the dishes again, her back faced me.

"I came to check on you, mama," I said slowly walking into the kitchen keeping my distance from her.

She'd lost so much weight and appeared frail. I remember when I lived here she appeared larger than life despite her short stature. I know now it was just her demeaning presence.

"I don't know why you're here to check on me. I'm not a

drug dealer and I don't associate with them. So you can just turn your black ass around and go to wherever you came from," she continued as she rinsed a few forks and spoons and placed them on the dish rack.

"Mama…," I said swallowing my saliva already feeling the tears filling up within the wells of my eyes. "How…I mean…how come you don't love me? What can I do to make you love me? I'll be getting married soon, and I wanted you to be there. I want you to be a part of my life."

"Married?" she laughed. "Nobody in their right mind would marry you, Parade. What are you talking about?"

That hurt. In fact, it crushed me. I knew it would be a long time before I could get over those words. What's worse was that she was possibly right. Smokes had no intentions on marrying me. Her words were knives. It wasn't until recently that I started to disbelieve some of the things she said to me when I was younger. And I knew it would take me many more years to get over these words now. Still, I couldn't leave, not without knowing why she hates me. Her only daughter. Her only child.

"Mama…is it my fault you don't love me? Was I not a good daughter? If I wasn't I'm sorry mama. I always loved you. I still love you now." She ignored me, and that hurt far more than anything she could've said.

"Mama…please talk to me! Be decent to me for once in your life. I love you mama!" I sobbed. "Talk to me please!"

Still nothing. My head dropped. I was done. She made it clear that she didn't love me. *Ever*. There was nothing more I could do. I would have to live my life, without a mother. Without the one woman I should be able to count on. I took one last look at the back of my mother's body. It would be the last memory I had of her. The last memory I would have of a life full of hatred.

I walked toward the door with my head down, and then I heard, "Parade."

My entire body trembled. She didn't call me a black bitch

or a whore this time. She called me by my birth name. Yet I was so frightened of rejection that I couldn't face her.

"Yes, mama," I said looking at the front door. I was sure her back was still faced me too.

"It…It's not your fault," she stuttered as I heard the dishes clinging. "It's mine. Just give me some time to clear things out in my head. Okay?"

"Y…yes, mama!" I cried heavily. "Thank you sooo much, mama!"

Her words lifted years of pain off of my heart. And I ran out the door before she'd have a chance to change her mind. My mother didn't know it, but with the small ounce of hope she gave me, she also gave me back part of my life.

"What exactly do I have to do, Smokes?" I asked him as we sat side by side on the couch. "And why is she here?" I asked pointing at Sweets.

"I'm here because I'm a friend, Parade." She sounded sincere. "Stop thinkin' I'm out to get you cause I'm not. Trust me, I'm more on your side than you think."

She'd said that before many times and I never knew what that meant. I looked at Smokes and for a second, my mind went back to the conversation I had with Jay. He pleaded with me to be two steps ahead at *all* times. I mean, why would Smokes have me do anything illegal if he truly loved me?

"Smokes…can I talk to you alone?"

He looked at Sweets before he looked at me and I became enraged. Who was she and what was this hold she had over him? I was supposed to be his so-called fiancé. And trust…now that I had Jay, all I really wanted was out, but he wouldn't let me. So I decided to test what was really going on.

"Parade, I'm not the enemy," Sweets continued.

"Baby," I said rubbing his knee. "Please, just five min-

utes…*alone*." He looked at her, shook his head and she left the room. When the bitch was gone, I addressed him. "Listen…I've been thinking, I want to be with you. And I'm ready to be with you forever. I know we've gone through a lot over the past few days and I'm sorry. I don't want anybody but you, not even Jay. I'm also ready to be down for you and do anything you need from me."

"I know, Parade. But what's really up?"

"When are we getting married?" I asked him softly. "I'm ready to be your wife…*now*." He turned away from me, cleared his throat and looked back at me. It was the first time I noticed his apprehension.

"Soon…let's just get past this thing we gotta take care of first. We need money for a wedding and right now the funds are low."

"Baby, I want to marry you in a few weeks. I don't need a big wedding anymore. All that's important to me is you. Just me…you and a couple of our close friends at the Justice of the Peace will do me just fine. Will you marry me, baby?" I hoped he wouldn't say yes and it would backfire on me.

"I will, but not now, Parade. Soon though. Okay?" he said pushing me off.

"Okay." Jay was definitely right.

After our short convo he didn't call Sweets back and told me what he wanted. What he wanted me to do was crazy and dangerous. I was supposed to board a plane to the Dominican Republic with over $100,000 strapped to my body. Once there someone was going to meet me to collect the funds. Once the funds were received they would arrange for the dope to be in the states within 48 hours. He promised me that I'd never have to touch any drugs but I didn't believe him. All I knew was that there was no way I'd be able to go through with it. I hadn't realized things could get so involved. I didn't see a positive outcome in sight, and although I listened, I had one thing on my mind, get-

ting myself out of this scenario and ridding myself of Smokes once and for all

.

Daffany

Finally I had some moments alone and trust me it was hard. Miss Wayne wouldn't leave my side for three days straight! And although I managed to stretch out the last bit of heroin I stuck in my pussy, it wasn't easy. Now I was out. Although I got high only four hours ago, my body craved it. And the way my baby moved I knew it craved it too. But I told myself, once it was gone, I wasn't smoking anymore. I didn't want to go through anything near what I went through when that man violently raped and tortured me for eight hours while his wife was at work.

Taking a bag of my dirty clothes down to the Laundromat, I decided to wash on my own. Just to get out of the house and breathe some fresh air. It was the first time I left the apartment since I got here and I needed a break. My baby moved some more and I rubbed my tummy and smiled. I really do want to be a better mother, and this time, I really am going to try.

When I walked down the stairs, and toward the Laundromat, I felt off balance. A part of me wanted to run out into the streets to get high again. While the other part of me wanted to conquer my fear, and push forward. Getting high was always in the back of my mind and this time was no different.

I had just emptied my dark clothes in the washer when *he* walked in. I had heard Keith calling the house day in and day out trying to beg Miss Wayne to get rid of me but Miss Wayne hung up every time.

"What do you want?" I asked as he walked fully in the Laundromat wearing his cop's uniform. "Miss Wayne ain't here." I brushed past him, placed the laundry basket on the floor, opened the next washer and threw my whites inside. Then I poured in some liquid Gain detergent afterwards placing two dollar's worth of quarters into the machine. He stayed there watching the entire thing like it was a movie.

"I know he's not here…I finally was able to get him on the phone," he said hopping on the dryer like a bitch eyeballing me. "So I came to see you instead. You don't mind me seeing you do you? After everything we've been through."

"What do you want, Keith?" I grabbed my basket and placing the detergent inside. "I don't want any trouble."

"You don't want any trouble?" he mocked. "You ain't nothin' but trouble. But today I'm gonna be easy. You won. You got what you wanted. Me out the picture for good."

"I didn't want you out of the picture. I just wanted you to leave me alone." I told him wondering if now would be a good time to exit.

"Well let's put all of that behind us. I'm just here to make sure you're cool with your recovery."

"I am," I lied. "Don't worry about me." I held my belly with one hand, and held onto the laundry basket with the other. Rubbing my stomach I was preparing to leave when he called me.

"Daffany, I got something for you," he told me coolly. "Something I know you really want."

I turned around and saw a bag filled with heroin and a pipe. Instantly I felt all types of tingles running through me. I dropped the basket and was pulled to him like a magnet. The thick green liquid from the Gain bottle poured ino the basket and onto the floor. But I couldn't stop until I was directly in front of him. Sweat dressed my forehead and my mouth salivated.

"Look at you…you ain't nothin' but a junky, bitch!" I

stood in front of him feenin'. All I could think about was injecting the powerful drug. I wasn't concerned with what he said to me or what he did.

"P…please…I…I want it sooo bad," I begged him. I had been craving all day but my body went into full ache mode now. "Please give it to me." I whined as I reached for it.

He hit my hand and said, "What are you willing to do for it?"

"Anything…I'm willing to do anything," I rubbed my hand over my anxious body.

He hopped off the machine, placed a spoon, a lighter, the syringe and a shoestring on the dryer and stared at me with lustful eyes.

"Anything huh?" he repeated. "I wonder what that really means."

I didn't look at him. My eyes remained fixated on my addiction. I wanted it. I needed it. So badly my pussy tingled. He pushed me further toward the dryer and it took me a second to realize he was tugging at my pants. Pressing my stomach against the dryer he ripped off my panties and entered my body…raw. While he pushed in and out of me, I grabbed everything and shot up. The sexual feeling mixed with the high lifted me to a higher place. Why did I ever think I could change? Once a junky always a junky and tonight, I just wanted to get high.

Miss Wayne found me passed out. When I came to, he was rocking me in his arms on the couch. The look on his face terrified me and I knew it was all my fault. I can't remember how I got from the Laundromat here, all I remember was that *it* happened. I had violated my friendship by having sex with his boyfriend and in my stupor, I recalled telling Miss Wayne about it. I guess it was important to me not to infect him. But right now, all I wanted was outta here.

"Are you okay, baby?" he asked me wiping his tears. I nodded yes although I wasn't. I just wanted to get out and run away from the shame I felt inside.

"Everything is going to be okay, Miss Daffany," he promised me. "But you have to be strong. You can't keep runnin' out there in them streets and gettin' high. You gonna kill yourself and your baby. When I found you downstairs in the laundry room I almost died thinking you were dead. You're not healthy, Miss Daffany. We got to get you healthy, honey."

I nodded in understanding. But for some reason, all I could think about was leaving, finding Carmen, along with my next high. I liked who I was high. I didn't worry about things or cared about people. Seeing how he felt hurt. Badly, and it didn't feel good.

"I have to leave…I'm sorry," I told him trying to rise to my feet from the sofa. "Please."

"Miss Daffany, I can't let you go. We have to work this out. Everything will be alright…you'll see. You just need to know you have people out here who care about you."

"What people? The only one who gives a fuck about me is you, Miss Wayne." I sat up straight. "Parade, doesn't care no more and I can't say I blame her."

"That's not true. Miss Parade, loves you it just hard for her to see you like this. But isn't my love enough?"

Silence.

"Let me help you, Miss Daffany. You've been out there fucking around too long. Look at you."

Right before I could respond someone knocked at the door. "Stay right there, honey." He rose up. "Let me get rid of whoever this is." When he opened the door Keith was behind it. Miss Wayne cocked back and hit him so hard in the face, he hit the floor. "That's the first blow you'll get," he stooped down and waved his finger in his face. "The next blow will happen once you visit the doctors and find out you have HIV!"

Without waiting for his answer he slammed the door shut. Keith yelled out in pain because his foot was in the way and Miss Wayne kicked it out of the door's path and slammed it again.

"I'm gonna kick your ass you fuckin', slut!" Keith yelled from the hallway.

"Go fuck your mamma!" Miss Wayne responded.

When he was done he walked back toward the kitchen. While thoughts of what I was going to do once I got free ran through my mind, Miss Wayne got on the phone. He walked away and I couldn't hear what he was saying. But I could tell he was deep in conversation. Who was he calling?

Miss Wayne

"Miss Parade, I need you to come over here," I said in a low voice as I watched Miss Daffany watch me from the sofa. I turned my back so she couldn't hear what I was saying.

"You call me out of the blue and I don't hear from you in weeks and now you want me to come over?" she said sarcastically. "Well forget about it."

"Miss Parade…have I always been there for you? When you needed me?" Her silence told me everything I already knew. "Well I need *you* now. Can you be decent enough to come over here? Please. I need your help and I'm not askin' twice."

She paused for a long moment and said, "I'm on my way."

I hung up the phone and exhaled. Thank God, because what I needed now was a miracle. I was about to do something that could cause Miss Daffany a lot of pain, but I didn't see any another way. I was not going to lose her to the drug that already claimed so much of her life already. And if I wasn't careful, and caught it now, it would claim the baby's life too. With Miss Parade on the way, I was about to commit the ultimate. Kidnapping.

Miss Parade came about a hour later and I knew she took her time on purpose. But I didn't care, at least she was here.

"What do you want," she told me after walking in. "I got somewhere to go later so I can't stay long."

"Thanks for coming, Miss Parade," I said slowly trying to avoid an argument. "But I'm gonna need your help a little longer. So you'll have to cancel your plans."

"Well," she said shrugging her shoulders. "Are you gonna tell me what's this about or what? Since you're asking me to stop everything for you when you stop nothing for me."

"Come with me," I said pulling her by the hand. Her shoes made a squeaking sound as they scratched the floor.

"Stop rushing me! I'm coming…damn!"

When we opened the door to my bedroom, Miss Daffany's arms and legs were tied to the ends of my bed as she kicked wildly. I know this was a little extreme, but everything else I did wasn't working. I had to go all the way if I wanted to save her and the baby's life.

"What the fuck is going on?" she asked screaming at me while looking at Miss Daffany. I walked over to the bed, sat down and tried to talk over Miss Daffany who was yelling and going wild.

"Miss Wayne, let me go! Why are you doing this to me? You're hurting me!" Miss Daffany cried out. My heart pang to hear her like that.

"We are family," I said to Miss Parade as I dipped a rag in a bucket of cool water I had next to the bed to wipe away Miss Daffany's sweat and tears. It looked like a scene from the movie *Exorcist*. "I need you to help me detox Miss Daffany. I'm tired of her going through this. Today I found her passed out in the laundry room. *And* she had sex with Keith. I don't know any other way to help her, Miss Parade. If I did I would take it."

"Why not just send her to the hospital? They can do a better job of detoxing her than you can. Plus she's pregnant and you don't know what type of damage you'll do. Not to mention she has AID's! Come on, Miss Wayne, be smart about this shit! This

ain't nothin' like them shows you seen on TV. This shit is real and you could kill her."

"Let me go! I'm gonna stop messing with drugs! I promise!" Miss Daffany cried in the background. "Parade, tell him to let me go!"

"Miss Parade, if I let her go, that red bitch Carmen will get her hands on her again. And I can't have that. I have to save her life. And I'm asking you, my oldest friend, to help me." I didn't realize I was crying nor was I trying too in order to gain sympathy. Everything I was saying was coming from the heart. We were family but lately we were acting like enemies.

Miss Parade took one look at me, then at Miss Daffany and said, "This ain't my problem. I got problems of my own. I'm sorry."

She walked toward my bedroom door, without looking back and walked out of it. My head dropped and my spirit was crushed. I sobbed heavily over Miss Daffany's pleas for me to let her go. How was I going to take care of her on my own? She needed love and I needed help. With nothing else to do, I decided to talk to God.

Trying to block out Miss Daffany's cries I said, "Father…I know You don't recognize me. I'm a gay man whose been living a not so legal lifestyle. I cheat, steal and do what I can for myself. I'm sure there are probably people who deserve Your attention *way* more than I do. But I'd give my life to save Miss Daffany and her baby. She has never had a break…ever. I'm asking for Your help, Father God. I don't know what else to do. I'm lost and don't know where else to turn. If this is not Your will, I'll give up on it all. I just need a sign. Please. Amen."

Five seconds later Miss Parade came back in, threw her purse on the floor and sat on the other side of the bed. Looking at me she wiped her tears and held Miss Daffany's hand who surprisingly enough, stopped fighting.

"You're an, ass!" she told me. "But I am too, and I can't

leave you two alone. If you're going to jail I'm going with you. I'm probably gonna die tomorrow anyway." I wondered what *die tomorrow* meant but thought it was her inner diva coming out and crying for attention again. "We're family. I love you."

"I love you too," I winked happy God had answered my prayers so quickly. "Are you ready?"

"Yeah…I am." She sighed. "Let's get started."

Parade

It had been a week since I called home. I'd been at Miss Wayne's the entire time. My phone rang off the hook with Smokes and Jay trying to find me. Eventually I just let their calls drain my battery until it cut off altogether.

Detoxing Daffany was the hardest thing I've ever had to do in my life. Daffany went through every kind of body pang imaginable. The first 6 hours she began to sweat profusely and we had to untie her arms because she was in so much discomfort. After 24 hours, she cried constantly while holding her stomach in pain. I was worried that she'd lose the baby and begged Miss Wayne to let me take her to the hospital but he stood strong. So I waited and watched her go from sweating claiming to be hot to wrapping her body up due to feeling so cold. We forced small pieces of fruit down her throat for the baby's sake. Some she kept down most she didn't.

Miss Wayne told me things would be okay and we took shifts spending time with her. After a few days, the pain didn't seem as bad but she started complaining that her vagina was extra sensitive and that her legs cramped. Then right before our eyes she went back to the shivers and complaining of being cold. I hated seeing her like that, but the fact that she would be well after everything was said and done pushed me forward.

And now, finally, she was out of the bedroom and eating

cereal at the kitchen table. We had plans to take her to the doctor's later to check on her health. And we still weren't going to leave her side. One of us had pledged to be with her at all times.

"Hungry?" Miss Wayne asked me as he fussed over breakfast in the kitchen.

"Yeah…I'll take some eggs," I told him smiling at Daffany. "Welcome back, girl!" I nudged her shoulders. She was thin and looked like she'd been through hell, but for the first time in a long time, I saw my friend again. She smiled, looked at the bowl of cereal in front of her and then dropped the spoon. Then she started crying.

"I…I…am sooo sorry for what I put, ya'll through," she wept. "I know this don't mean nothing right now, but I'm gonna stay clean. For myself…my baby…and, yall."

Miss Wayne rushed by her side and I did too. "Listen, baby," he said rubbing her back. "It don't matter what you did. All that matters is where you're going. You're clean, and today we gonna take you to the doctor, find out about the baby and go on with our lives. There's no need for apologies."

"Yeah…it's all downhill from here," I told her. "The rest should be easy."

"I love, yall," she said.

I kissed her cheek and smiled. If we talked about this anymore we all were going to be crying. I can't believe I was about to leave her side. She was my friend. One of my dearest friends. If I could lay in the same bed with a murderer, the least I could do was forgive someone who always had my back.

"Miss Wayne, can I use your cell phone charger?" I asked remembering I hadn't talked to my sweetheart in a while. "I wanna call Jay right quick." When I stood up, I put my belt with the word Parade in rhinestones on. It had been lying in my lap.

"Jay?" Daffany questioned wiping her tears. "When did that happen?"

"I'll tell you everything later." I grabbed the charger from

Miss Wayne and plugged up my phone so it could power up. I saw fifty messages.

I ignored the voice mails and the text messages and tried to call Jay but he didn't answer his phone. Being away from him was the toughest part about everything. All I wanted to do was make him happy and go on with our lives. But I knew this thing with Smokes wouldn't go away easily. He'd proven to me the type of man he was and I knew what he was capable of. When I looked at a few of the texts, one of them hurt me so bad my heart ached.

Parade, I guess by now you've made your decision. And I can tell by the way you ignorin' my calls you ain't choose me. I just want you to know that I'm gonna always love you. I also want you to know that I'm changin' a lot of shit in my life and have made a decision to move to L.A. I need a change of pace. When you get this I won't answer your calls. I'm trying to move on so you can too. Take care, and I hope he makes you happy. He betta. Jay.

"What baby?" Miss Wayne asked rushing by my side. I guess my face said it all. I had lost the one man I loved. And I knew he was gone forever. But before I could say anything there was heavy beating on the door.

"Hold up," Miss Wayne said in his natural male voice. "Who the fuck beatin' at my door like they lost their fuckin' mind?!"

"It's me, girl," a feminine male voice called out from the other side. "Open this door. I know you got some new shit in there!"

Miss Wayne laughed when he heard the voice and said, "That probably ain't nobody but Miss Dayshawn's faggy ass. I'm supposed to be hookin' him up with some luggage for his trip to the Bahamas's next month. Let me get this right quick."

Daffany and I engaged in short conversation at the kitchen table while Miss Wayne opened the door. The thunder from the door being kicked open and Miss Wayne falling to the floor made me damn near pop out of my skin. Daffany jumped up against the wall and it was seconds before I was being snatched up. It was Zeeway.

"Bitch, get your shit and get the fuck up!" he told me grabbing me by my forearm. "Smokes been lookin' all over for ya ass!"

"Nigga, get your fuckin' hands off of me!" I told him as I used the side of my hand to hit him in the throat. "You must've bumped your fuckin' head touchin' me, nigga!"

Before I could get another blow in, Miss Wayne came running behnd him with a cast iron pan. Zeeway saw this and diverted his attention from me to handle Miss Wayne's muscular ass. But before Miss Wayne could reach him, he slipped on the spilled milk from Daffany's cereal bowl and busted his ass on the kitchen floor. Daffany continued to scream while I decided to do what I did best, whip this mothafucka's ass like he stole somethin'. I rushed his punk ass and caught him off guard. I knew once I had him it was a wrap! No man or woman could fuck with the way I wrecked.

"Nigga, you," I paused to hold his head under my arm, with my toes spread and pressed against the hardwood floor. "betta get the fuck…outta here…before…I punish your ass!" I must've gut punched him and stole him in his face several times before he realized what happened.

"You crazy ass, bitch!" he yelled trying to get away from me.

Some kind of way he got a hold of my neck and put my right arm behind my back as he held it firmly behind me. And because I knew how to use both hands in a fight, I twisted out of it using my elbow to punch him in the stomach again. I was just about to commence to beating his ass some more when he pulled out a gun.

"Bitch…," he said breathing heavily. "I should shoot

your fuckin' ass right now and tell that nigga it was a mistake!"

I bit my tongue even though I wasn't scared of his gun. I had a gun thrown in my face before and I'm still here. The only thing I worried about was Daffany and Miss Wayne. I didn't want them hurt because I got off on kicking this punk nigga's ass. So I decided to calm down, and leave without any altercations.

"Let's go, bitch before I murder your ass!" he demanded.

Before I left I looked at Miss Wayne who was rubbing his ankle. I hoped he didn't break it. Then I looked at Daffany and said, "I'm gonna be okay, guys. Trust me," I hoped it was true.

I went hesitantly and barefoot without anymore altercations. For now anyway.

I didn't talk while Zeeway took me toward Quincy Manor apartments in his royal blue Suburban. My arms remained folded against my stomach as I ignored everything he said.

"Yous a tough lil' black, bitch," he told me as he used one hand to rub his busted lip. "But I wonder how tough you gonna be when you take that trip." He laughed.

I just looked at him and rolled my eyes.

When we pulled up in the parking lot in the back of the development, I contemplated running but where was I going to go? My car was back at Miss Wayne's and Smokes would catch me and probably kill my mother and my friends.

"Get out," he demanded opening my car door. Once outside the truck, he pulled me by my forearm and I thought about beating his ass again.

"You betta be glad you got that gun, nigga cause I'd be kickin' your ass some more!" I warned.

"Put your hands on me again and I'ma make an excuse to Smokes on why ya ass is showin' up missin'. He wouldn't give a fuck anyway. It'll be one less bitch he gotta worry about."

"I wonder what the Dominicans would think since it's

obvious they want me there," I said smartly. He looked scared. "If he doin' all this I must be worth somethin'," I giggled.

"Bitch, bring your ass on!"

I allowed him to pull me toward the building as we walked hurriedly down some steps. Once we got to our destination, he knocked twice and the door opened wide. Another man I'd never seen before was inside. Nothing was in the apartment and all the blinds were drawn making it dark because the sun couldn't shine on the back part of the building. When someone finally cut the lights on, I saw Jay tied up on a chair and my heart dropped.

Not caring what anybody had to say, I rushed up to him and wrapped my arms around his neck. He was beat up so badly he sighed a little when I touched him.

"You okay, baby?" I asked even though he couldn't speak due to the duct tape covering his lips. He nodded yes but I knew he wasn't.

"He aight…but you ain't goin' be if you don't do what we ask you too," Zeeway promised.

Standing up straight I looked at Zeeway wanting to scratch his fuckin' eyes out! I hated him and everything he stood for. I also knew, once I boarded that plane with all that money attached to my body, I wasn't coming back home. I don't care what lie Smokes told me. My naïve days were over and I was growing smarter by the second. Everybody who has ever used me taught me a lesson in one way or another.

"What I gotta do?"

"You know what you gotta do," he told me. "And you'll have to see Smokes 'bout the details. I just wanted to bring you by here so you could see the severity of the situation," he laughed. "Now let's go."

I took one last look at Jay and broke away from Zeeway to hold him again. If he wanted to shoot me so be it. I had to say goodbye to the true love of my life because I didn't know when

I'd see him again. Or better yet, *if* I'd ever lay eyes on him again. The way it looked, we were both not going to make it.

"I love you, Jay," I cried confessing my love to him. "I've always loved you."

"I…mub..you moo," he said under the tape covering his lips.

"Stop with the chivalries and let's get the fuck outta here!" he said grabbing my arm.

One man stayed with Jay in the apartment as he rushed me outside. I sobbed thinking of the life we could've had now lost. How could I have been so stupid? I already knew what kind of man Smokes was yet I was going to marry him anyway. Just to have somebody to call my own. Just to have all of the riches I wanted when I was younger. I traded my soul for material things and was going to lose everything that really mattered in the process. Daffany was right about me. Lately I had become selfish. And if I could do it all over again, I would.

As I got in the car one thing ran through my mind. I can take this mothafucka. Taking one last look at him as he slid in the driver's seat, my thoughts were confirmed. He was a bitch ass nigga and I knew it. Here I was barefoot and angry. The only reason I hesitated on busting his shit was because of the gun he was holding. What if I got shot and nobody found out about Jay? I couldn't take the thought of something happening to him. But anything happening to Jay was what made me go for it.

The moment he placed one hand on the steering wheel preparing to pull off, I cocked my right hand back and as hard as I could, hit him in his cheek. The blood from his face splattered against the window as if it had left a spray bottle. Once it did that, I followed up with another blow. His eyes got wide like he was in a daze trying to figure out what happened. So before he could think straight, again I hit him with another blow. You would've thought after the last ass whippin' I gave him at Miss Wayne's, that he'd be smarter than to leave my hands free. And had

Smokes really known me, he would've told him too. Then again, I didn't really know Smokes, either. I was so caught up into getting back to Jay and dealing with the consequences later that I didn't see Zeeway coming for my neck with both hands.

"You black, bitch! Fuck this job I'm about to kill ya fuckin' ass and deal with Smokes later!" he continued squeezing my throat tightly.

My hands went wildly before landing on his face. My left finger nail dug into his nose and more of his blood escaped his body and rolled down his lip. He looked like he'd been in a war and in a manner of speaking, he had.

Although I was fighting, I could feel my throat getting tighter and I began to feel light headed. My world was floating and my soul felt like it was escaping. My eye lids were heavy and I suddenly felt a need to close them. And all of a sudden, nothing mattered. Not Jay, not Smokes and not my life. I was ready to give up on the fight of my life and leave this world for good.

And as soon as I gave up, I saw the driver's door swing open and a man yank Zeeway out of the door. Zeeway tried to fight him but the mysterious man, I didn't know, hit him over and over again with a closed fist until Zeeway lay weakly on the ground. Half of his body lay outside the truck while his feet remained inside.

"Hey…you betta get outta here," the stranger said breathing heavily looking down at Zeeway.

I rubbed my throat and looked at him strangely. Why did he help me and who was he? I was about to ask him his name until I saw the word Kelsi tatted on his right arm.

"W…why did you help me?" I asked rubbing my throat surprised I was still alive.

"I uuon't know. But unless you want me to change my mind, I suggest you get the fuck outta here before you be dealin' wit'your problems on your own again."

I didn't press the issue. Just got up and started moving.

Something about him seemed familiar. It was like we were cut from the same cloth. Once outside, I took one last look at my hero and ran away. I needed to call Miss Wayne to get some help. I don't even know why I didn't call the police first. But it didn't matter because by the time I dialed the first digit, three cop cars pulled up beside me. I started to run but my energy level was weak due to almost being killed.

"Get down or we'll shoot," they promised.

There were about ten cops pointing weapons at me and all I could do was comply. And when I got down, I was grabbed up and thrown in the back of a police car. What was going on, and what did they want from me? This day was going from piss to shit quick! I needed help.

Parade

The interrogation room was cold and drab and I was frustrated. They didn't even have the decency to tell me what was going on, or give me any shoes. It was like they were trying to keep me in suspense on purpose. Twenty minutes after I'd been brought in, the person who came through the door almost made me fall out of my chair.

"Hello, Parade…how are you?" she asked as she opened the door. Taking the seat directly across from me at the table, she smiled.

"What the fuck is going on?" I asked shocked to see her. She even had a badge hanging around her neck. "And who are you…really?"

She smiled again and I felt like knocking her teeth out of her mouth. I had Jay on my mind and wasn't in the playing mood.

"Well…for starters my name isn't Sweets. It's Essence. And I'm an undercover detective in the homicide division. I'm also working in conjunction with the FBI to bring down Smokes. We've been after him for quite some time now."

The room seemed off balance and I didn't know if I should be happy or sad. After all, she was basically telling me I wasn't in this thing alone. I hadn't even discussed my issue with Miss Wayne or Jay. I didn't want to get anybody more involved

than I already had. I guess that's what she meant when she said *she's more on my side than I realize.*

"What the fuck does any of this have to do with me?" I was trying to maintain control.

She smiled, and said, "More than you think. For starters, we want you to testify against Smokes. We have several charges stemming from the murder of your friend Sky Taylor to drug trafficking across state lines. He's in over his head now and all we need is your help. Silver has already conspired against him for a lighter sentence and your testimony would help tremendously."

I knew it! Silver was a bitch ass nigga all along! Still, hearing Sky's name in the same sentence as Smokes again made me feel ashamed. How could I betray her in death? I was willing to do anything to undue the wrong I'd done but I wasn't sure if testifying was it. I never was a snitch and I wasn't about to start now. Instead, I decided to present her with a little piece of evidence I had that nobody knew about. When Smokes broke down to me what I had to do, the day after my talk with Jay, I recorded the entire conversation. I took Jay's advice about being two steps ahead seriously. And now I was glad I did.

"I'm sorry. I have the code of the streets all in my blood and I won't be able to testify, but I recorded a conversation I had with him and it goes into detail about what he wanted me to do. You know…the night you were at the house and trying to eavesdrop. Would that be enough to bring him down?" The smile on her face told me everything I needed to know.

"It would be perfect! Where is it?" she questioned.

"At home. I hid it so he won't be able to find it."

"Great, we'll take you there to get it after we get the warrant back for his arrest. We should have it in a few minutes. I would've been able to record the conversation myself but you insisted that I leave. That's why I was so adamant about staying."

While she talked I thought about how cozy she was with Smokes and had a question of my own that needed to be answered.

"Did you sleep with him?" I blurted out.

"Let's just say I do what I have to for my shield."

I just smiled. As long as he was out of the way and I wouldn't be forced to do anything illegal. I was happy. Although I was partially relieved, Jay was still heavy on my mind. I needed to know what happened to him but was afraid to ask. Maybe I really didn't want to hear the truth. And then she said, "Before we leave, I have someone I want you to see."

She left for five minutes before returning with Jay. He was bruised and he limped a little but he was okay. I ran up to him and wrapped my hands around his neck. My baby was alive.

"I'll leave you two alone for a few minutes," she said walking toward the door. "Parade, thanks for everything."

"Sure!" I was excited to see my baby's face.

When she left I said, "I thought I lost you for good," I kissed his swollen and bruised lips.

"How you figure you were gonna get rid of me that easy?" he said wrapping his arms around my waist. Although in pain, he held me like not a bone on his body ached. He was definitely a trooper. "I told you, you had me for life."

"Then why were you going to move to L.A.?"

"I was gonna move to L.A. to get myself together, Parade. And it's still somethin' I wanna do. But it won't stop my love for you."

I was disappointed because I wanted him here with me. "So that means we really are through?"

"Naw…it means I hope you like the warm weather, cuz we moving together."

I laughed and kissed him again. "I was getting ready to say!" I was still caught up in the mood when I remembered something. "How did they know you were there?"

"Zeeway got that Onstar shit in his car. So they were able to track him. They woulda been found my ass a long time ago but

had trouble finding out what building I was in. I think they even went to Wayne's because he must've went there too."

"Yeah…we weren't at Miss Wayne's too long before we left and he took me to the apartment. I hope they lock his bitch ass under the jail."

"That nigga not goin' back to jail," Jay laughed.

"Why not? He was just involved in this shit as everybody else."

"They found his ass behind the wheel of his car dead. He must've got somebody else fucked up."

In all the drama I forgot about my friend Kelsi who saved my life. And I hoped in the future I'd be able to thank him, although I doubt it was about that with him. Real niggas do real shit.

For some reason, despite all the dismay, I felt content, relaxed, happy and most of all in love. With the possibility of my relationship with my mother being renewed, I could finally exhale, and live my life. To the fullest.

Smokes

Smokes walked around his home in hysterics. He couldn't reach Zeeway. He couldn't even find Tate, the man that held Jay at gunpoint. And most of all, he couldn't locate Parade. When his phone rang he hesitated at first because he knew who it was. Ace was not only expecting the cash Parade was to wear taped to her body, but she was also supposed to be sold as product in the sex trade.

"Today is your last day," Ace said. "If she doesn't get off that plane today, you might as well kill yourself."

"Fuck you, nigga!" Smokes said arrogantly knowing that all was lost anyway. He figured he might as well talk shit in his last hours.

"You gonna wish you didn't say that."

Without responding Smokes hung up. He was just getting ready to place one last call to find out what was going on when he heard a loud crashing noise at the front door followed by heaving running through his home. Could Ace make it here that quick? He thought. He looked out the window and saw cop cars everywhere. He was surrounded. He had two options. Go to jail or kill himself. If he went to jail, Ace would surely have him tortured before being murdered. But if he killed himself, he could go out smooth and choose his own fate.

So instead of panicking, he sat at this desk, threw his feet on top of it and lit one of his Cherry flavored Blunts. Then he

downed all of the Ciroc vodka he poured earlier in his glass.

"Freeze! Put your hands up!" one of the cops yelled after busting in his office door. Ten or eleven guns stayed pointed in his direction.

Smokes didn't budge, just laughed. When he moved to pull open his desk drawer they demanded he freeze again.

"You betta freeze before we shoot, mothafucka! It's over!" one cop yelled.

He was still laughing until he saw Sweet's face. Instantly the smile was removed when he saw the badge dangling around her neck. He had a snake in his mist the entire time and didn't know. Suddenly he wasn't as cool anymore but wasn't going to show it.

"I should've known you was a stank ass, bitch!" he spat.

"It's over, Smokes. Why don't you stand up and surrender? Make this smooth," Sweets replied.

"Fuck you, bitch," he yelled as he pulled out the gun from his drawer, put it under his chin, and blew his brains out. And just like that, it was over.

Everything.

Epilogue

The large blue beach sparkled under the Cancun sun. People ran barefoot over the yellow warm sand, playing, laughing and wading in the ice blue water. Mexico couldn't be more beautiful at *La Costa Resorts* then it was right then.

"Look at, Shanay," Miss Wayne fussed as he laid stretched out on one of the lawn chairs. His purple toe nail polish glistened while he sported his yellow female bathing suit. Even though he was far too muscular for it, he didn't care. As far as he was concerned, he was the hottest thing on the beach. "She has all that sand in her bikini bottoms. Shanay!" he yelled directing his attention to Daffany's baby. "Bring yourself over here!"

Shanay wobbled over to Miss Wayne knowing she was in for something. Although she was a two year old baby, she could always tell by the tone of his voice when she was in trouble.

"Leave that baby alone," Daffany laughed sipping on a Pina Colada. The royal blue two piece bikini she sported looked sexy on her fit body. She was taking care of herself and hadn't used drugs in over two years. And because she was taking the cocktails for her HIV disease, she was feeling much better too. "You worse than me."

Miss Wayne shook his head and lifted the baby onto his lap. Once there, he brushed her off with his bare hands. He took his God mother status to a whole nother level. He was always so worried about her.

"He is something else," Parade added wearing the same black and rhinestone bathing suit she wore the day she and Jay made *real* love. "But I'm sure she knows he loves her."

"I sure do," Miss Wayne confirmed. "And I'm gonna do the same thing when you pop that one out of your belly."

Parade laughed and rubbed her three month pregnant belly with her left hand which was covered with her wedding ring.

"Doubt it," Jay interrupted kissing Parade on her cheek. They were all on their lawn chairs next to each other looking at the sparkling water. "I got this over here!"

"Boy, bye!" Miss Wayne joked. "You family now so you might as well find out that I get's into *everybody's* business. Including your wife's."

Jay didn't respond, just reached over and kissed his beautiful wife on the lips.

Miss Wayne, Daffany, Parade and Jay decided it was time to take a vacation. Life for the friends couldn't be better. They all moved to L.A. and purchased a beautiful brick apartment building with the cash Parade was smart enough to tuck away while living with Smokes and the money Jay had stashed from being in the drug game so long.

Parade opened up a make-up store while Daffany and Miss Wayne sold clothes in their boutique. Jay on the other hand got involved in real estate and bought and sold property in and around L.A. To say they were well off was an understatement.

Things had gotten better for the friends, but *really* good for Parade. Although her relationship with her mother was not perfect, she could at least call and speak to her without being emotionally broken down. Parade knew her mother was trying to do better, and that's all she could ask for. Parade knew it would take some time for them to be close, but she was willing to work at it. Her father on the other hand loved her and called her as often as he could.

Outside of everything, Parade's marriage to Jay was the

best thing that happened to her. For two years he whined and dined her and showed in his actions how much he loved her. He never disrespected her or called her out of her name. He took care of her and proudly showed her around to his new friends in L.A. as the love of his life. He even got his mother to be cordial, after Parade apologized for beating her ass. They were certainly happy together. Life was great. Life was perfect. And it was all because they fought for love. In the end Parade learned that there was no such thing as being *Black and Ugly*. And if anything, black couldn't be more beautiful.

THE CARTEL COLLECTION

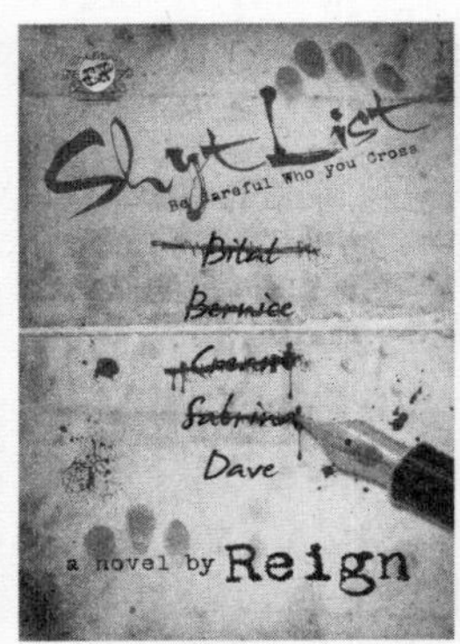

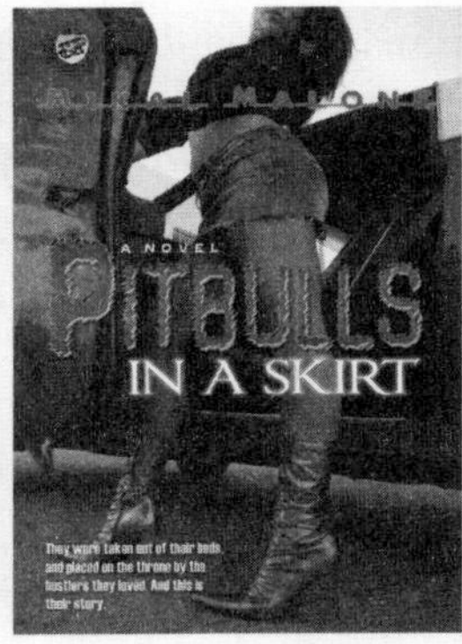

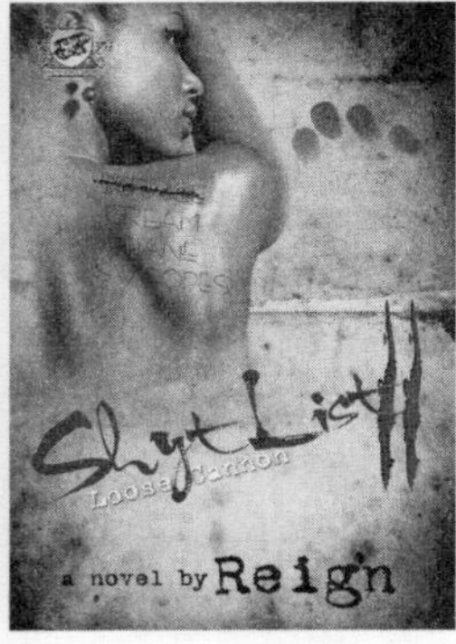

Cartel Publications Order Form

www.thecartelpublications.com

Prisoners Receive Books For $10.00. All Orders Must Still Include Shipping Fees *Per* Book.

Titles	***Select The Novels You Want Below***	***Fee***
Shyt List	________________	$15.00
Pitbulls In A Skirt	________________	$15.00
Victoria's Secret	________________	$15.00
Poison	________________	$15.00
Hell Razor Honeys	________________	$15.00
A Hustler's Son 2	________________	$15.00
Black And Ugly As Ever	___________	$15.00

Please add $2.00 per book for shipping and handling.

Total: $____________

Mailing Address

The Cartel Publications * P.O. Box 486 * Owings Mills * MD * 21117

Name: ____________________________________

Address: ____________________________________

City/State: ____________________________________

Contact #: ____________________________________

Email: ____________________________________

Special Note:
Please allow 5-7 business days for delivery. The Cartel is not responsible for prison orders rejected. **We accept stamps**.

Wanna Become A Street Team Member?

Complete The Application Below

Name:

____

Address:

____

Prisoners Are Welcome 2 Join The Team, Too!

For Every Three Books You Sell, You'll Get One Book Free. Just Have The Customer Complete The Order Form and Write Your Name & Address In The Bottom Left-hand Corner.

OBD
ODDBALLDSGN
OUT OF THE ORDINARY YET EXTRAORDINARY
301.325.6460 WWW.ODDBALLDSGN.COM
WEB DESIGN BOOK COVERS CD COVERS FLYERS LOGOS POSTERS BOOKMARKS PHOTO EDITING EVENT TICKETS BUSINESS CARDS
500 BUSINESS CARDS FREE
PURCHASE 500 BUSINESS CARDS AND GET ANOTHER 500 FREE
10% OFF WEB SITE DESIGN
500 POSTCARDS FREE
ORDER BOOK COVER DESIGN AND GET 500 POSTCARDS FREE
"It's nice to have someone you can count on, especially for all of my last minute jobs!!"
-Lana Rae, CEO KIS Promotions
"I've never seen anyone work that fast"
-Iesha Brown CEO, Outta DaBlue Publishing

If I've learned anything since running the Cartel, I've learned that my readers are Everything! I thank you for supporting me, my authors, and our company.

-T.Styles
President
&
CEO
The Cartel Publications